Christmas at Hart's Lodge

REBEKAH R. GANIERE

ISBN: 978-1-63300-062-9
ISBN: 978-1-63300-063-6

Cover art by VWZDesigns.com

Dedication

For my Mom.
Who got me loving Sweet Christmas Romance Movies

Chapter One

G abrielle circled the small round table decked out in pristine white linen tablecloth and Swarovski crystal goblets. The wind stayed to a minimum under the drapey white canopy swathed in twinkling miniature Christmas lights.

She scanned every item on the table as she lit the tall candelabras making sure everything was in its place.

Her cellphone beeped and she pushed her blonde hair from her eyes as she pulled out her phone. Her head whipped up and she scanned the park. Across the green, on the street curb, a white horse drawn carriage stopped and a young man stepped out and helped a pretty brunette from her seat.

Gabrielle rushed away from the table stopping just long enough to fix a drooping red rose in the center of the table and straighten a fork. She pushed the button on the side of her headset.

"They're here."

"We're ready," Matt replied.

Gabrielle ran from the canopy and ducked around a large hedge just as the young man led his astonished date to the table and pulled the chair out for her before sitting in his own seat.

Gabrielle peeked over the bushes. "Matt, now."

Matt, dapperly dressed as a footman from an old Victorian manor house, approached the table with a bottle of champagne and offered it to the couple. The young woman giggled as nervousness played across her features. The young man nodded and Matt opened the bottle and poured some into each flute.

In perfect orchestration Gabrielle was back on her headset. She was the chess master making the pieces move around the board in a beautiful waltz- but only for everyone else.

"Johan, get ready. In three... two... one."

Matt bowed and strolled away just as Johan arrived with a tray full of two plates of food.

"Oh, my goodness," said the young woman. "Is that from Chez Marina?"

Her date smiled and nodded.

"I can't believe you did all this. It's the most amazing thing anyone has ever done for me. Thank you so much."

"You're worth every penny."

She took his hand in hers and smiled. Gabrielle took a moment to enjoy the happiness she'd brought the couple. But it was only tempered by her own lack of success in her love life. She called it her 'Love Curse'. It'd started in junior high and had continued all the way up to two years prior when her fiancé had informed her that he wanted to marry her, but also wanted to continue living in a open relationship-something she hadn't realized they'd been doing.

If she couldn't have it for herself, at least she could make it happen for others, was her motto. But in the quiet moments when she caught a glimpse of the happiness shared by two people truly in love, she couldn't help but feel a prick of jealousy. Her mother had always taught her to be grateful for her blessings as well as the blessings others received, but every once in a while, she couldn't help but wish she had more.

Gabrielle sighed and swallowed hard. *No time for that.* She needed to focus. Her job wasn't finished yet.

"Sebastian are you ready? You're up as soon as Johan is done serving."

"I'm on it Boss."

Johan walked away as Sebastian, Gabrielle's college wingman and now a violinist with a large symphony, strolled onto the scene playing Pachelbel Cannon in D Major. Perfection. If she was ever going to have a night where someone would get down on one knee and propose, this would be her heaven.

Thirty minutes later Gabrielle stood in the same spot stamping her feet in the chilly air. She pulled her coat tighter around herself and looked around the hedge. The couple were just finishing their meal when the client spotted Gabrielle and nodded.

"All right guys, time to bring this home. Matt, more champagne and Johan, desert. Go now."

Everyone took their places and Johan set dessert on the table.

The woman took a bite of her torte to find a ring inside. She squealed. Gabrielle's client got down on one knee. His date squealed again and flung herself at him.

Gabrielle smiled. Just like the rest of the night, Matt poured more champagne as Sebastian moved in with more music. Her job was done.

"Give them as long as they want and then tear it all down. Great job guys. Another successful night."

Gabrielle strolled off and headed for her car. She'd managed to help one more couple find love. That made over thirty-four in the last two years. Now, if she could just find one for herself.

Chapter Two

G abrielle opened the door to her small yet comfy apartment and walked inside, as exhaustion settled around her.

"Evie, I'm home." Gabrielle set her coat and purse on the kitchen table before taking off her headset and rolling her shoulders.

She groaned looking at the kitchen table that she used as a workstation. Against the rest of the well-organized apartment, it stuck out like a hoarder's paradise. Covered in look books, swatches, brochures, vendor cards and anything else she might need to set up the perfect date. She reminded herself yet again that she really needed to find a better system for keeping things organized.

"Evie, are you back yet?" she called. But no one

answered. She glanced at the clock above the stove. Ten thirty. Her roommate and best friend should've been home already.

Gabrielle straightened the table enough to find her laptop. She opened it and while it booted up she headed for the kitchen. Thumbing through her sparse fridge, she pulled out a yogurt and a bottle of juice. She mentally put shopping on her to do list before her next job started.

Gabrielle ambled back to the table and looked over her emails. One popped up marked Urgent: CANCELLATION.

She scanned the cancellation and issued a response to the unlucky guy who'd just been broken up with. She added her usual dose of 'shoulder to cry on' along with a heaping spoonful of 'it'll happen in the right time'. Though she could use the money, part of her was glad for the cancellation. She could definitely use a break. Christmas was in less than a week and a half away and by the time New Years hit, she'd be booked solid through Valentines. The holidays always brought engagements.

Gabrielle closed her laptop and stretched. She had so much to do to prepare for Christmas. She hadn't even started shopping for gifts for her parents.

As if the umbilical cord was still attached, her

phone rang and the name Mom popped up on the screen.

"Hey." Gabrielle grabbed her laptop, walked across the front room and down the hall to her bedroom. She set her computer on her bed, shucked off her shoes, and began to undress.

"Hey sweetie. How did it go?"

"Another successful engagement."

"You're so good."

Gabrielle sighed and pulled a pair of pajamas out of her dresser. "For other people I am."

"Your Prince Charming will show up when you least expect it."

She dragged on her pajamas and sat heavily on her bed. "Well, I never expect it anymore so..."

"Don't be like that. Just because one guy couldn't see your worth-"

"The one guy I was supposed to *marry*."

"Well, you saved yourself from that one, didn't you?"

Silence filled the line for a moment. Her mom and dad had been sweethearts who'd been married straight after senior year before he went into the Navy. Gabrielle had spent her high school years waiting to find the same kind of match, but none ever arrived. Then as college year one turned into college year two, she started to worry that maybe she'd never find the right guy. But just as her hopes had hit an all-time low, she'd met Derrick. And after six months of dating, six months of engagement, and his sudden announcement that he'd been seeing someone else the entire time, she'd sworn to stay strictly in the friend zone with men. And that's where she'd continued to stay for the last three years.

"It doesn't matter anyway," Gabrielle said. "I don't have time for a relationship. My business takes everything I have. The majority of new businesses fail within the first year. I've made it to two, but if I want to make it to three I need to up my game."

"Is business going okay?"

"Actually, I just had a cancellation." Gabrielle threw on a smile. "But that means I'll be able to come in this weekend and stay the whole week with you."

"That would be great. We have a lot to do before Christmas Eve."

"I know. I won't let dad and the kids down."

"I'm just looking forward to you being home and relaxing for a few days. You've worked so hard to get your business off the ground." Her mom paused.

The sound of going home and relaxing for a few days was as good as her mom saying they were going to vacation at a spa for a month.

"You know your dad and I would be happy to-"

"No Mom. You and Dad paid for my schooling and I'm the one who chose to leave and start my own business. I need to do this on my own. And you're right. I really could use a few days to regroup."

"We're really looking forward to seeing you. And..."

Uh-oh. "And?"

"There's a new recruiter at your dad's office who is just the cutest-"

"Thanks, but I'm just fine on my own."

"Are you though? You just said-"

"That I have no time for a relationship. Or did you miss that part?" Gabrielle plopped down on her bed. "Tell Dad I say hi."

"He already has the checkers board set up and waiting." Her mom always took the change of subject in stride.

"Tell him I'm bringing my game face. I'll let you know for sure by Thursday, when I'll be in."

"Sounds good. Get some sleep. You deserve it."

"Love you Mom."

"Love you too, sweetie."

Gabrielle hung up and pulled down the covers on her bed. Picking up her laptop she went to her Facebook page. She had all 5 star ratings and there was a new photo of the couple from the park on her page with an endorsement. She closed her laptop unsure of how she felt about having no imminent obligations. One look at her bank account told her that she couldn't afford to have just lost that client. She looked around her room and sighed. Despite what she'd said to her mom, deep inside she really did just want to find her own happily ever after. It was true Gabrielle didn't have the time, but more than that she didn't have the heart to try again only to end up being hurt by her Love Curse.

GABRIELLE AWOKE AN HOUR LATER TO THE slamming of the front door .

"Yes, Chantel, I'm on it.... Of course... first thing in the morning... I will... Yup... No problem." Evie's voice floated down the hall.

Gabrielle looked at the time on her phone. *Midnight.* She shook her head.

Evie's footsteps grew louder as she continuing to placate her boss.

Gabrielle sat up as Evie plopped onto her bed and rolled her eyes.

Gabrielle thought about ripping the phone from Evie's hands, but instead she mouthed. "Hang up."

Evie smiled at her and held up a finger.

"It's midnight!"

Evie nodded. "Yes, Chantel, it will all be ready for the shoot first thing in the morning... Sure thing. Yup. I'll upload all the photos from tonight's shoot before I go to bed. Okay. I'll see you in the morning... Non-fat double latte with hazelnut milk, two and a half squirts of vanilla... and a vegan strawberry Danish... I always remember... You have a great night too. Chow."

Evie dropped on her bed and sighed.

"Evie-"

"I know. I know. I would have been home hours ago but we went downtown to that new club and it was crazy. I stayed to help make sure she got the right photos with the right people and stuff."

Gabrielle shook her head. "I will never understand living that kind of life. Being a social advertiser."

"Influencer. People pay her to show up at their places and to use their products. Do you realize that as of two days ago she has more followers than all of the Kardash-" Evie stopped and covered her mouth. "Chantel has forbidden me from mentioning their name. *That family* put together? The girl is a mega star!"

Gabrielle chuckled and headed toward the bathroom. "She's an instafamous socialite who spends her time posting perfect videos about her fake fabulous life while pretending that she got it through hard work instead of a trust fund."

"That was mean."

Gabrielle stopped and turned back. "You're right. I'm sorry. I'm cranky."

"What's up?"

Gabrielle covered her face with her hands. What was up? What wasn't up? Her love life for one thing. That wasn't up. That wasn't even lying down. At the moment it was dead in a locker at the bottom of an ocean for all she knew. Right along with her finances.

"My couple cancelled for this weekend," she finally said.

"I'm sorry."

Gabrielle headed into the bathroom. "I've poured everything I have into this company. I love what I do. I've worked so hard I just need that one break to go from barely paying my bills to really exploding. If I can't bring in more clients I'm going to lose everything and end up under a mountain of debt."

Gabrielle grabbed a band for her hair and had just put her hair up in a ponytail when Evie hugged her.

"I'm sorry, Gabs. I wish there was something I could do to-" Evie pushed Gabrielle to arm's length. "Oh my gosh!"

"What?"

Evie's eyes lit up as bright as the Christmas tree in the lobby of their apartment building. "Oh my gosh! Oh my gosh!"

Gabrielle couldn't help the smile that broke across her face despite the fear of what Evie had brewing in her mind. "What? What?"

"Okay. I can't promise anything but I overheard Chantel talking to her best friend Mandy today about how she wanted to setup a fun romantic weekend with her boyfriend and propose to him."

"Chantel wants to propose to her boyfriend?" *How very modern of her.*

"She's been waiting for months for him to propose and then she finally decided that the best way to get the proposal of her dreams was to do it herself. And the only way for her to get the picture-perfect proposal is to have the best proposal master in the universe to set it up for her!"

"That sounds like a lot of pressure."

Evie snorted. "You just said that you needed a break to explode your business. What better way than to have the world's most internet famous face as a client?"

Gabrielle's gut twisted. "That would be totally amazing but-"

Evie waved her off. "But nothing. We've been best friends since we were four and you've always been the one to help me. Let me help you for once."

It was true... if she could secure someone as famous as Chantel for a client it could be just the boost her company needed. But the risk if something went wrong could be catastrophic... not that anything had ever gone wrong before. *Knock on wood.*

"Well, I guess you do owe me," Gabrielle said. "I mean you did ask me to deliver a love note to Shawn Jones in third grade which ended up with me getting punched in the eye by Beth Snapper."

"Absolutely. So, you just make sure that when I call you tomorrow you are ready to meet up. And be sure to wear something professional."

Gabrielle looked at her pajamas. "What? She's not into unicorns?"

Evie laughed and skipped back to her bed, throwing a pillow at Gabrielle.

Gabrielle caught it. "Fine. But I am not bringing her ridiculous coffee and wheatgrass Danishes."

"You won't even have to bring her a tofu egg salad sandwich."

Gabrielle wrinkled her nose. "Is that a thing?"

"It is for her."

Chapter Three

Gabrielle waited on Chantel's couch. She looked at her phone. Ten twenty. Their meeting had been scheduled for ten. Gabrielle blew out a breath and took in the space for the millionth time. The posh apartment could be the winner of a Better Homes and Gardens Christmas decorating contest. Decked out in bright white Christmas decor, it sparkled and gleamed from the marble floors to the mini chandelier. A white tree adorned in silver and crystal balls- looking like it cost more than everything in Gabrielle's whole apartment- stood proudly in the corner.

Only the backdrop and lighting set up behind the couch detracted from the winter wonderland. On the coffee table lay a dozen or so different products lined up awaiting Chantel's stamp of approval.

Evie rushed out of the back of the apartment, into the kitchen and turned on the espresso maker.

"She'll be just a minute. We've almost finished picking out the photos for posting today."

"Photos of what?"

"The club last night. Apparently, there was someone photobombing in the background."

Gabrielle shook her head as Evie disappeared again. She got up and crossed to a fireplace mantel. Photos of Chantel with friends, at parties, and one of her kissing a guy on the cheek sat on the mantel. She picked up the picture and looked at Chantel with the handsome blond man holding a set of car keys and sitting on the hood of a Tesla.

"Must be nice." Gabrielle fought against the jealousy that threatened to burrow inside her.

"Hiiiiii!"

Gabrielle turned to see the socialite epitome of a rich girl. A former cheerleader and popular, trust fund baby with an award-winning smile and a beauty queen body.

Gabrielle set the photo on the mantel as Chantel crossed and pulled her into a surprisingly real hug. Not a fake pat on your back hug. But the kind of hug that made a person feel truly connected to another.

"You must be the proposal wrangler I've heard so much about. I'm so happy to meet you," Chantel said.

Gabrielle looked to Evie for help as she patted Chantel on the back.

"Go with it," Evie mouthed.

Chantel released Gabrielle and threw her a smile. She squeezed Gabrielle's hands. "Thank you so much for coming on such short notice." She let go of Gabrielle and curled up on the couch.

Gabrielle sat on a plush cream chair across from her. "I prefer Perfect Date Specialist."

Chantel picked up the first product and looked at it. "Right. Evie has been talking about you all morning and saying you can help me get the perfect date with my beau."

"I specialize in perfect dates."

Chantel put down the product and picked up a bottle of perfume. "Perfect. So, I want to marry my boyfriend but he's a bit on the old-fashioned side. We've been together for quite a while and I'm ready to make him my forever perfect partner."

"You want a romantic date to help him see you're the one?" Gabrielle asked.

Chantel sprayed the perfume and sniffed it. She coughed and put it on the coffee table as Evie headed over with some wipes and handed them to Chantel.

"Oh no. He knows I'm the one. I just need him to see that now's the time. We were voted the cutest couple on Instachat. My followers have made it clear he's the one they want me to be with."

Chantel grabbed her phone and flipped through something. "Photos with my guy? Almost a million likes."

She flipped her phone toward Gabrielle so fast Gabrielle didn't catch the photo.

"Photos of me with my coffee? Only three hundred thousand." Chantel stopped and squealed. "That's it! A proposal would be perfect posting material for Christmas and New Years. I could get up to two or three million likes all season long and then if it starts trending... oh man... don't get me started."

Gabrielle looked between Evie and Chantel. "Okay." *No pressure or anything.*

"Evie has told me a million times that you have a one hundred percent success rate. You do this right for me and I'll pay you three times your normal rate. Not only that but I'll make sure to give you a huge shout out on my live feed I'll be videoing when I propose. I'll get you so much business you'll never have to advertise again."

Gabrielle fought to keep her eyes from bugging out of her head, but she couldn't suppress the huge smile that crept across her face. Three times her normal rate? That would pay her rent for months. Maybe even make her able to hire an accountant or an extra pair of hands.

Chantel picked up a lip gloss and smoothed it on her lips. She smacked them together a few times and then handed it to Evie.

"This one."

Evie nodded and moved all of the other products off the table as Chantel positioned herself on the couch.

She smiled at Gabrielle. "Should I take that as a yes?"

Without thinking Gabrielle blurted, "Yes!"

Chantel chuckled. "Perfect. So, I need you to go up to Hart's Lodge ahead of me. I have to do some last-minute shopping and finish getting some things together and we can have our date. Say... Saturday?"

"Wait, Hart's Lodge? Up in Park Hills?" That was a two hour drive into the mountains. She didn't know anyone up there. No servers. No vendors. Nothing.

And so close to Christmas she was sure her normal guys wouldn't make the drive.

"It's so cute up there so... naturish. With trees and snow and stuff."

Gabrielle pulled out her phone and googled Hart's Lodge. "You want me to go up there and just find some outdoorsy kind of things." She scrolled through the first page on Google, but nothing showed up besides their address, phone number and some satellite photos.

"Sure. He loves outdoor stuff."

Gabrielle flipped through all the photos she could find of the lodge and the town. "Uh... okay. I can do that."

"Are you sure? I need this to be perfect and if you can't-"

Gabrielle stopped scrolling and her head whipped up. "No. I can. I promise. I won't let you down. I just need to get some clothes-"

Chantel waved her hand. "I called you an Uber already. It's downstairs waiting. Evie can pack your stuff up and send it to you by carrier later."

Evie handed Chantel the lip gloss and then turned on the photo lights, pulled out her phone and started snapping dozens of photos.

Gabrielle watched for a moment before realizing that the conversation was over.

"Oh... uh... okay. Well, I'll just go then."

Chantel stopped posing and waved to Gabrielle. "Thanks hun. I'm super excited. Can't wait to see what you can do."

Gabrielle opened her mouth but wasn't sure how to respond.

Chantel looked back at camera. "Okay let's live stream now."

Gabrielle showed herself to the door and made a mental note to tell Evie just how much she owed her. Nervousness crept over her as she headed out the door. She had to get this right. If she didn't her business was as good as dead. But if she did...

GABRIELLE SAT IN THE BACK OF THE UBER, watching the city drift away and the mountains come into view. As the trees thickened and the white snow-caps drew closer, anxiety rooted inside her. What had she just agreed to? She wasn't one that usually jumped into doing things without thinking them through, thoroughly. But the money and possible free PR was so enticing.

"Gaby, are you there?"

"What? Yes mom." She pushed her anxiety away. "No, I won't miss Christmas, but I won't be coming early either. I picked up a last-minute client."

"Well, I know your dad will be sorry not to spend as much time playing checkers with us, but we understand."

Gabrielle looked out her window at the winding road. Snow drifted from the skies and she suddenly wished she'd brought some warmer clothes.

"Hopefully I'll be there by Monday." Her cell phone crackled. "I better go, the cell signal is getting spotty up here."

"Okay honey... warm. Love..."

The line went dead. Gabrielle looked at her phone and then put it in her lap.

THE MOUNTAINS ENGULFED HER AND THE CAR. She could practically smell the fresh air through the tinted windows. Her heart grew heavy as she realized though she lived close to nature, she hadn't been out of the city in forever. Her business had completely overtaken her life. In the small moment of analysis she realized she'd not been out with friends in forever. She'd not even gone to the movies or dancing in over six months. She couldn't remember the last time she'd eaten something that didn't come in a box. And she hadn't had a haircut in... well from the state of her split ends, quite a while. Maybe after she got this job finished she could spend a bit of time doing something fun, even if it was alone.

Chapter Four

Gabrielle exited the Uber in front of a beautiful mountain lodge. Greenery and Christmas decor adorned the entrance. A huge red bow surrounded fresh green swags and twinkling white icicles. A light smattering of snow had begun to stick to the ground, making Gabrielle smile. She took a deep breath and reveled in the scent of fresh pine and crisp air. It was as if she stood in the middle of a life size Christmas snow globe.

Families and couples walked up the stone steps. The sounds of happy chatter and bright Christmas music floated out to meet her.

The Uber pulled away and Gabrielle stood for a moment allowing the ambiance of the magical place to recharge her batteries. If this was the place she needed to make a man propose to Chantel, maybe it was possible after all.

Gabrielle entered the lodge, again struck by the warm Christmas decor. The scent of warm apple cider made her stomach grumble. She hadn't eaten all morning. Looking at her watch she realized it was past lunchtime.

Piano music played beautifully from another room. Gabrielle started for it when the woman behind the front desk called to her.

"Hi. Can I help you?"

Gabrielle turned to the front desk. An ageless woman with a youthful warm smile thanked a family of four and then looked to Gabrielle again.

Gabrielle walked toward her, and spotted her nametag which read, Patty.

"Hi Patty. I'm Gabrielle Miller and I need a room please."

"Do you have a reservation?"

"I don't. But I only need it for a couple of days. Until Sunday at the latest."

Patty frowned and shook her head. "I'm sorry hun, but we are all booked for Christmas."

Gabrielle's gut clenched. "Don't you have anything?"

"I'm afraid not. There's another lodge about fifteen

minutes away but I'm pretty sure they're booked as well."

Ugh! Of course, Chantel wouldn't bother to make a reservation or even see if she could get one for Gabrielle. But Gabrielle wasn't above begging.

"I really need a room. You see I have this business helping people and my client wants to do this special thing here with her boyfriend and I promised I'd set it up for her-"

"I would really like to help you. You seem sweet, but unless we get a cancellation there's nothing I can do."

"Hey, Patty. What's going on?"

Gabrielle looked over to see a tall handsome guy with stylish brown hair and a fitted red flannel shirt walk up to the counter and grab a piece of candy from the candy dish. He looked over at Gabrielle and smiled.

"Hi," he said.

"This young lady is looking for a room. I told her we're booked solid for the next two weeks," said Patty.

"I see." He extended his hand to Gabrielle. "Theo Hart."

A flush of heat passed through Gabrielle as she reached out and shook his hand. "Gabrielle Miller."

He popped the candy into his mouth. "Gabrielle, I like that."

They smiled at each other until Gabrielle noticed Patty looking on. Her cheeks heated and she dropped her gaze. *Focus, girl. He's cute, but you can't screw this up. Business first.*

"So, we're usually booked solid for the holidays, but I might have something you could have. Not that it will be pristine though." Theo looked to Patty. "Has the accident room been fixed yet?"

"Accident room?" Gabrielle wasn't sure she liked the sound of that.

"It's not finished, if that's what you're asking," said Patty.

"But the new beds have been put in, right? And the walls have been painted?"

"Yes, but it still smells and there are no curtains yet or console or-"

"I'll take it," Gabrielle blurted. If there was a bed that was all she needed. Hell, she'd take a cot in the storage closet if she had to.

Patty stared at her incredulously. "Are you sure?"

"Yes." Before anyone could change their mind Gabrielle dug into her purse and pulled out her credit card. She didn't even bother to ask the price. With Chantel paying her, it really didn't matter.

Theo kept his gaze on her. "Half price. Since it's not quite up to Hart standard."

Gabrielle fought the butterflies fluttering in her stomach. Theo Hart might be hot and rugged as they come but she was not about to stir that pot. *Remember your curse? You can't afford to have that kick in with the someone while you are trying to use their lodge to build your future.*

"Thank you so much. You have no idea how much I appreciate this," she said.

"You are very welcome." Theo smiled, showing off a dimple on his right cheek.

Okay, he really needed to stop being so adorable.

Patty handed Gabrielle her credit card and the room key along with the paperwork.

"Let me help you with your bags," said Theo.

Dang. Hot and chivalrous too. Could he be any harder to resist? "Oh... I uh... They aren't here yet. They should be here this evening."

Theo nodded. "Well let me show you to your room then."

She should tell him thank you but no. She should walk away and focus on the task at hand.

"Thank you," was what came out of her mouth.

They walked together out of the lobby with Gabrielle kicking herself for not telling him no. But even as her brain told her no, her heart and body told her yes.

They walked past a large open common room where people lounged in front of a large fireplace, read and played games. It was beautifully peaceful to not be bombarded by phones and computers and televisions.

"So why do you call it the 'accident room'?" she asked as they continued down the hall.

"Uh... my... friend, was up here a few months back and they put too many aromatherapy candles up in the room, fell asleep and caught the room on fire."

"Wow!"

Theo chuckled.

"Yeah. She kept saying it was an accident. Even though we'd warned her not to light the candles."

"That's terrible. Thank heavens no one was hurt."

Theo stopped by a room with a 'Do Not Enter' sign on the door.

"So, this is me?"

"This is you."

Gabrielle put the key in the door and opened it. She walked inside and coughed covering her nose at the smell. Two beds sat unmade with the mattresses still in plastic. The walls were devoid of any pictures and there was no tv, dresser, or anything besides the beds. Even so it was the smell that was the most overpowering.

"Sorry. It still smells like-"

"Burnt roses?" she said.

"Before it smelled like a crematorium."

Gabrielle laughed and looked at him. "You go to mortuaries often to know what that smells like?"

He laughed. "Actually, I don't."

She walked over to the window without curtains and looked outside. The snow had begun to blanket the ground. The falling snow obscuring her view of everything and bringing with it an isolating silence.

"I'll see if I can round up something to cover the window with as well as some towels and linens and stuff."

Gabrielle turned from the window. "Thank you."

Theo headed for the door but then stopped and scratched his head before shoving his hands in his pockets. "You don't happen to want to grab some lunch in about an hour do you?"

Gabrielle's skin flushed with heat. She wrapped her arms around herself. He was cute, but she couldn't afford to get sidetracked.

"Well, I am here for work and I need to get started-"

Theo smiled and held up his hands. "Say no more. I get it." He continued to the door again.

"But I could stand to eat," she blurted. "And, maybe I could pick your brain about things to do here at the Lodge? Or you could make me a list?"

Theo turned and smiled again. "Sure. I'd be happy to help. I'll find you those items and be back in a bit."

Gabrielle's phone rang as Theo left. She looked at it and then answered.

"Evie?"

"Did you make it okay?"

Gabrielle sat on the bed. "Just got here. When will you guys be here?"

Evie sighed. "I have no idea. Chantel is shopping now. We could be a while."

"Well, no rush. I have plenty of work ahead of me."

"Okay. Hey, have you-" The phone broke up.

"What? I didn't hear you."

There was no answer.

"Evie?... Evie?" The phone disconnected.

Gabrielle looked at her phone but she had barely half a bar. She stood and walked to the window to find the snow growing steadily deeper. *Well, that's not good.*

A KNOCK SOUNDED ON THE DOOR. "Housekeeping."

Theo held up a set of blankets, sheets and towels when she answered.

"I didn't find any curtains but I got a shower curtain and figured we could hang that up."

"Sounds great," she said.

He set the blankets and sheets on one of the beds and walked with the shower curtain to the window and held it up as Gabrielle put the sheets on the bed.

"You don't need to do that. I can have house-keeping come and make the bed," he said.

She looked at him sideways. "I thought you were housekeeping."

"True enough."

He set the shower curtain on the small table and helped her make the bed.

"So, you said you were here for work? What kind of work? I don't recognize you as a return guest."

"You remember all the guests that come here?" She tucked in a corner of the fitted sheet.

"I grew up in the lodge. Most of our customers have been coming here with their families for decades."

"Really?"

He shrugged. "It's a blessing and a curse."

"How so?"

"We have a lot of repeat customers but not a lot of the younger crowd. And we're only really open during the winter months."

"Why no younger crowd?"

"No Wi-Fi. Spotty cell signal. No hip restaurant or swanky clubs. It doesn't bother me, I prefer it that way.

They go up to the ski lodge up the hill to get those things."

"Yeah, I noticed you guys didn't even have a website."

"We prefer to stay old school."

There was old school and then there was old fashioned. Those were two different things. "So, what is there to do here?"

Theo tossed her a pillow and she slipped the pillowcase on it.

"Outdoor stuff. Snowmobiling. Sledding. Tubing. Cross country. Star gazing. "

"Oh, you mean stuff that doesn't involve using more than just your fingers?"

Theo chuckled. "Exactly."

Gabrielle liked his laugh. It was open and friendly and his eyes crinkled in the corners. He was the perfect combination of metrosexual pretty boy, and hometown rugged lumberjack. She squished the flutters building inside her and reminded herself that she wasn't there to flirt.

Chapter Five

T he budding stirrings inside when he looked at her conflicted Theo. Gabrielle was so different than the girls he usually went for. Sweet and funny with a great sense of adventure. And she was hands down one of the most beautiful women he'd ever seen. With her long golden hair and big blue eyes. But she hadn't tried to cover herself in with makeup, to make herself look like a totally different person, he liked that. He didn't know many other girls who would have taken the accident room in the condition it was in- not that he knew many girls that weren't obsessed with mundane things like their looks, their clothes and the latest trends.

Damn. He was once again struck by just how arrogant and materialistic his life had become since moving to the city. It was why he'd taken time off and came home for Christmas. After taking a couple bad stock tips, as well as a string of dead end relationships he needed to get his crap together.

"So do you work here year-round?" Gabrielle asked

"No. I work in the city. I come up a couple times a month and do the books for my parents."

"You're a bookkeeper?"

"CPA for a large firm. And you?"

"I'm a special date planner."

Theo chuckled. "A what?"

"A special date planner. It's like a wedding planner only for dates."

He shook his head. "And people pay you for that?"

She stopped and her mouth dropped open in mock offense. "You'd be surprised how hard it is for some people to be romantic."

"I probably would." It never ceased to surprise him what people would pay for. But then again his ex would have paid someone just to pee for her if it had been possible.

They walked into the lobby and Patty looked up from her desk before racing over to Theo.

"They're here."

Theo looked at his watch. It was barely noon. "Already?"

"They're unloading now."

Theo turned to Gabrielle. "Will you excuse me for a moment?"

She shrugged. "Of course."

Theo rushed out the door to a limousine sitting out front. A distinguished older couple stood by the vehicle as a driver unloaded their bags.

"Mr. and Mrs. Wentworth how great to see you." Theo bounded down the stairs.

The couple turned and smiled. Mr. Wentworth held out his hand and Theo shook it.

"Theo, how are you son?"

"Very good, sir."

Mrs. Wentworth leaned in and kissed him on the cheek while wrapping him in a hug. She smelled of Chanel No. 5 as she had every year since he was three years old.

"Hello sweet boy. How are your parents?"

"Great as always. They can't wait to see you."

The driver carried the bags up the steps and then hopped back in the car.

"Thank you, Arthur," Mrs. Wentworth called. "You know when to come back?"

Arthur nodded. "Yes, Ma'am. I will see you on the twenty-sixth."

An adorably dimpled young boy leaned out the window.

"Are you sure you can't come with us, Grandpa?" he called.

The Wentworth's son Willis poked his head out of the window. "Preston, Grandma and Grandpa have no interest in coming skiing with us."

"I'm a bit old to go skiing buddy. But you'll be back in a few days and we'll spend some time together for Christmas all right?" replied Mr. Wentworth.

"What about you Grandma? You're not too old."

Mrs. Wentworth chuckled and walked to the window. She leaned in and kissed Preston on the cheek. "Thank you for that, Lovie. I'll see you in a few days. I have a big Christmas surprise for you."

Sadness drooped Preston's angelic features as he sat back in his seat.

"Don't do anything fun you two," Willis called.

"Don't forget to get the Milestone proposal finished," Mr. Wentworth retorted.

"I won't, Dad." Willis motioned the driver to go.

Mrs. Wentworth blew Preston a kiss before the vehicle pulled away.

For the first time Theo found himself feeling bad for the boy. With divorced parents, and a father always working or socializing, and a mother who was too busy flying all over the world with the fashion business, he wondered if Preston might not have more fun staying with his grandparents for his Christmas break than up at the fancy ski lodge where he was bound to spend most of his time alone or with his nanny. It wasn't Theo's place to ask though.

"Come on. Let's get you settled." Theo and Patty picked up the bags and carried them into the lobby where Gabrielle waited.

Theo's parents descended the staircase wearing matching ugly Christmas sweaters, and headed for them.

"Dan, Jenny, so great to see you," said Theo's father.

"Hello Ronald. Margery." Mrs. Wentworth hugged them in turn.

Theo's mom spotted him with the Wentworths' bags. "Theo, give those to your dad. We'll get the Wentworth's situated."

Theo set the bags down and shook Daniel's hand again before locating Gabrielle by the check in counter watching him.

He crossed to her. "Food?"

"Please."

.   .   .

Theo and Gabrielle sat at a table looking over the menu. Not that Theo needed to look at a menu. It hadn't changed in twenty years and he already knew what he wanted.

"So, who was that couple you helped?" she asked.

"The Wentworths? They've been coming every year since I was a kid. It's always the same. They show up on the nineteenth and stay through the twenty-sixth. Same room, same routine, same everything."

She smiled. "That's how I like to picture my clients when I see them get engaged."

The waitress brought their drinks and they ordered.

Theo sipped his cola. "What do you mean?"

"I like to try and picture them thirty, forty, fifty years down the road. Still together. Holding hands. Surrounded by grandkids. I like to think that in some small way I helped make that happen."

Theo chuckled. "I love that you're optimistic like that. In today's world it's hard to find women who believe in anything more than a starter marriage."

She snorted. "I think maybe you're hanging around the wrong women."

She wasn't incorrect. It was just one more of the reasons he'd come home for an extended vacation.

"How did you get into that business?" he asked. "I've never heard of anything like it."

"In college I found myself helping out friends when they had an anniversary coming up or they wanted to propose, things like that. Soon word got out and people began paying me to help them. I found I liked it a lot more than what I'd been studying so I quit school and started my business."

"What were you studying?"

Her cheeks tinged with a beautiful shade of pink and she twirled the straw in her drink. "Criminal justice."

"Really?"

She smiled, making the corners of her eyes crinkle. "What? Can you not see me as a police officer?"

He tried to picture her five foot nothing self chasing down a criminal with a smile and a wink. "No. No, I can't."

"Me neither."

They both laughed and she ran her fingers through her long straight honey-colored hair, making it shower down over her shoulders.

"Are you crafting a perfect date up here?"

"I am," she said.

Their food arrived and the waitress set it down.

"My client specifically requested this lodge. I

figured I'd pick your brain to see what there is to offer. Then after we eat maybe I'll take a walk around. Make some notes on places I think are romantic. Maybe talk to the chef if possible and see what they can come up with for food ideas. Basically, get a feel for the place and what it has to offer."

Theo bit into his burger. He had a lot to do before Christmas, but something inside him just didn't want to leave Gabrielle's company. Her genuine charm and easy air made him feel more comfortable than he had in a long time. And kept his mind from trying to figure out whether or not to take his old partners to court for fraud.

"I wouldn't mind showing you, if you want."

She stopped mixing her soup and looked at him, her eyes conflicted. "I wouldn't want to take you away from your responsibilities and your family time."

"Trust me, the responsibilities aren't that big and I get plenty of family time."

If he was being honest, he was avoiding his parents at the moment. His mom was on a never-ending rampage to marry him off. If she saw him with Gabrielle, maybe he could get through his vacation without having to hear about it from her every waking moment.

"Uh..." Her eyebrows drew together and he got the

feeling his offer had made her uncomfortable for some reason.

"When do your clients come in?" he asked, trying to change the subject.

"I'm not exactly sure. The woman that hired me should be here by Friday. She wanted the date on Saturday. I am assuming the same goes for her boyfriend."

"Is it their anniversary or something?"

"Not... exactly. She wants him to propose. Apparently, he's been dragging his feet and she's hoping that a romantic date will help show him they are meant to be."

Theo's gut clenched. He used to date a girl who'd tried to manipulate him like that. Good thing he'd gotten rid of her a few months prior.

"Don't you think that's kind of cheating?" he finally asked. "I mean... isn't that kind of manipulative?"

Gabrielle's eyebrows drew together as she sipped her drink. "How so?"

"Some guy thinks he's getting this awesome date but in actuality the girl has ulterior motives."

"Can't the same be said when a woman is proposed to?"

She had a point. Most guys did usually do something super special and romantic to propose to their girl but... somehow the idea of it being the other way around rang disingenuous. Maybe he was jaded because of what he'd been through. Or maybe he just saw things in a different light now.

"To be honest, I've never done something like this before. It's kind of a special circumstance," she said.

"In what way?"

"Well, my client-"

"Theo!"

Theo's mom and dad walked to the table and Theo tried to deflect the barrage of questions he knew would be aimed his direction.

"Hey, Mom. Did the Wentworths get settled okay?"

"As always."

"Great."

His mom stood at the side of the table looking between him and Gabrielle. He was not going to get out of this one unless he ran out of the lodge.

"Mom, Dad. This is Gabrielle. She's just here for a few days to set up a date."

"How interesting," said his dad. "I'm Ronald."

"And I'm Margery. It's very nice to meet you."

Gabrielle smiled. "You too. You have a beautiful lodge."

"We like it," said his mom. She paused and Theo could practically hear all the questions buzzing around in her brain. He was about to try and head her off at the pass when she said, "It is so nice to meet you, Gabrielle. You're so different from the girls Theo usually dates."

Gabrielle looked at him. "Oh, we're not-"

"Nice. Wholesome. No cell phone in sight." His mom laughed out loud and again Gabrielle's gazed turned to him.

Theo's face flushed and he coughed. "Uh, thanks for that. Don't you and dad have somewhere to be? Something else you could be doing? Anything else you could be doing?"

His dad nodded and grabbed his mom by the arm. "We won't keep you."

"But honey, I want to-"

His dad interrupted his mom by dragging her away from the table.

Theo kept his eyes on his burger as he took a large bite and chewed extremely slowly. He could feel Gabrielle's gaze on him, but he didn't look up.

"So, you usually bring other girls up here huh?"

He took a large gulp of soda and tried to think of something to say.

A small smile crept across her face. "Good thing I'm not like them. They sound absolutely terrible."

They both burst out laughing and he couldn't help the feeling of once again being completely at ease with her. Like they'd known each other for years.

Chapter Six

G abrielle had finally agreed to let Theo show her around the property, but only because it would save her time. The back of the lodge had several small groups of people. Some drinking coffee, wassail, or hot cocoa and watching kids make snowmen. Others snowshoed off toward the woods. There were even several older kids sledding down a hill. But of all the people she noticed were in playing and drinking, only a handful appeared to be under fifty.

"There's so much to do here," she said.

"We bring in piles of fresh snow every morning but..." Theo looked skyward and stuck out his hand. "We might not need to for a few days."

"What do you mean?"

His thick eyebrows smashed together. "Didn't you hear about the huge storm coming in?"

A wave of panic settled in her chest. "No. Can you excuse me for a moment?"

"Sure."

Gabrielle pulled out her phone and dialed Evie as she walked to the edge of the sledding hill. She watched the kids slide down as the phone crackled but rang.

"Hello?"

"Did you know there's a snowstorm coming in?" Gabrielle bit her cheek. She didn't want them coming in early and having her be unprepared, but at the same time she didn't want to get stuck there and not make it home for Christmas.

"When?" asked Evie.

Theo walked over and showed her his phone. She groaned. The storm was already on its way.

"Today. Tonight."

Evie sighed. "Seriously?"

The sounds of women giggling and chattering floated through the phone.

Gabrielle shook her head. "When are you guys coming?"

"At this rate? After-"

Gabrielle stopped walking. "What?"

"I'm- I hope... Chantel is... the perfect outfit...now."

"What? Evie? I can't understand you."

Not good. This is not good.

"Looks like the storm...tonight but...by Saturday. We'll come...Saturday and the date...evening and you can still make it out...to your parents' by Monday."

Gabrielle was pretty sure she got the gist of what Evie was trying to say. "All right. But I need to get to my folks by Monday. No matter what-"

The line went dead. Gabrielle looked at it and then shoved it in her pocket.

"Problem?" asked Theo.

"Well, from what I heard, I think my client most likely isn't coming in until Saturday now. But it's fine. It gives me three days to get things worked out. I can leave when the date is done and be at my parents' by Monday. No problem."

They walked together a few steps to the cocoa stand.

"Wow. You have this down to a science."

"I just like being prepared."

Theo chuckled as he poured cocoa into two cups. "You and my dad would get along great. He believes in being prepared too." He handed one to Gabrielle.

She stared at it for a moment. "Wait."

Gabrielle took both cups, poured out twenty five percent of the liquid and then put them on the table. She took creamer and poured it a good portion into them. Then she added a heap of marshmallows and a candy cane.

She handed one to Theo and he took a sip.

A broad smile lit up his face. "Wow. That's so much better."

"That's only partly how my mom makes it." She sipped her own cup. "You don't have the other secret ingredients she usually uses."

"Well maybe I'll have to have you make me some with your special ingredient."

"I'll have to see if you have it in your kitchen."

"So why do you have to be home by Monday?"

Gabrielle leaned against the cocoa cart. "Every year my dad plays Santa and I play his elf and we go down to the battered women's shelter and hand out gifts to the kids. We've been doing it since I was little. We've never missed a year. Not even the year my dad had a heart attack. He insisted on going there, even though he had to go in a wheelchair. We decorated it to looks like a sleigh."

Theo watched her for a moment, making Gabrielle blush and look away.

Gabrielle and Theo moved to the sled hill again and watched the kids for several minutes. She fought against the sensations running through her. Theo was hot, and sweet. All the things she had been looking for in a guy, back when she'd been looking. She found herself attracted to him. And if she had to be stuck at the lodge for an extra day or two, there were worse guys to be stuck with. *No. She wasn't stuck, she was working. Remember the huge client who could change your business forever? Yeah, we can't screw that up.*

But... what could it hurt if she used Theo's knowledge of the lodge to help her find the best things to do for Chantel's special date. It wouldn't be like wasting time with him it would be like... having an assistant. A hot assistant who knew everything she needed to know and could save her lots of time. When she thought about it, not spending time with him would be just stupid. She'd have to do more work herself when she could just take him up on his offer to help her. He had offered, hadn't he?

"I'm supposed to go pick out a Christmas tree for the sitting room. Do you want to come with? For recon purposes of course. It would help you get to see more of the property," Theo offered.

See, right there. He was offering to help.

"Oh, thank you but I think I need to do some more recon on the place and then sit down and start making a game plan."

"But what good is making a plan on paper if you don't really experience things we have to offer? It's like going to France and then just reading about the Louvre."

He had a point.

She sipped her cocoa. "You're not just trying to lure me into the woods so you can chop me into bits, are you?"

Theo laughed, but then dropped his laugh. "No promises."

Gabrielle smiled. The woods could be something worth checking out. Maybe if she found a great spot with a nice view she could plan something for Chantel there on Saturday night.

"Okay. But I carry the axe."

Gabrielle stomped through the soft snow. She'd never been snowshoeing before and though it was awkward and difficult, she enjoyed the experience. She kept her eyes on Theo who walked ahead of her pulling a red sled behind him. She tried to imagine Chantel snowshoeing through the woods in her bright high heels. Nope that would definitely not be an activity she would enjoy, she could check snowshoeing off the list of things to do. Maybe there was a nice look out spot closer to the Lodge.

Gabrielle was about to ask when Theo stopped and dropped the rope to the sled. Theo slung off his backpack and pulled out a thermos and handed it to her and then pulled out two cups.

"It sure is beautiful out here. And so peaceful. I almost hate to disturb it," said Gabrielle.

"It's one of the reasons I love coming home. The outside world just fades away and you can really get back to the way things used to be. It's real up here. The people are real up here too."

He stood and undid the lid of the thermos, pouring each of them a cup of soup. Gabrielle blew on her cup before sipping it.

"What do you mean?"

Theo looked around. "You know. Before cellphones and social media and smart watches. When people were people not names on a screen and photoshopped photos that don't even look like the real person."

"I take it you aren't a big fan of the media age?"

"It serves its purpose as long as it doesn't become someone's purpose. Believe me, I used to be the same as all the rest. Posting staged photos. Pretending my life was perfect. Hopping around town. Looking like I was living the high life. But in actuality, I was lonelier down there surrounded by people than I ever have been up here. And swimming in debt." He paused and chuckled. "Sorry. Didn't mean to make that sound like a pity party. So what about you? Do you have 'in a relationship' as your status online?"

Gabrielle snorted. "Is 'cursed in love' a status option?"

"What?" His brow furrowed.

She waved him off. "Nothing. If I had a status it would be more like, *it's complicated*. At least that's what my ex would say."

His eyebrows creased together. "You don't seem complicated."

She opened her mouth but stopped. She hadn't talked about her breakup with anyone besides her parents and Evie. "I didn't think I was, but apparently me wanting him to be monogamous both while we were engaged and after we were married made me complicated."

"Wow. Okay, so secret girlfriends are where you draw the line, good to know." Theo cracked a smile making Gabrielle smile in return. They finished their soup and then continued with their trek in the woods.

"What about you?" she asked.

An uneasy smile crossed his face. "I was in a relationship but... I realized that we no longer wanted the same things and I backed off. To be honest, she's probably moved on to some picture-perfect guy with a great smile, great hair and never a speck of dirt under his nails."

"That's terrible."

"More like a relief to be honest."

Gabrielle tried not to laugh. He was going to just love having Chantel and her boyfriend in his lodge in a few days. She made a mental note to make sure he was nowhere to be seen when Chantel and her boyfriend were having their date.

"Don't get me wrong. She's a good person. She and I just want different things out of life. She likes things organized and planned out. I like things spontaneous and real. She loves her posh, sterile apartment with all the amenities and I like-"

"Your cozy rugged mountain retreat." She cocked an eyebrow at him and he threw her a dimple inducing smile.

"Exactly."

"I'm not a fan of people being able to get a hold of

me wherever I go," she said. "But when you own a startup business it's a necessary evil."

Theo looked abashed "Oh, I wasn't meaning you."

"I know. But I get what you mean. My best friend works for a woman like that. A million followers on whatever app. People she doesn't even know approve her every move."

"Exactly. A few months ago I closed all my social media accounts except one. I realized that the people whose opinions really matter are the ones I see in person, not a one-inch photo in a status feed whom I've never met."

"You closed all your accounts? Even I'm not there yet."

He eyed her for a moment. "You might. Or you might not. I think social media has some great benefits but I've seen the downside too. But honestly, I just don't think I'm interesting enough to have anything worth sharing." He pulled out an axe. "This is a pretty good place."

"To chop me up?"

He chuckled. "Nah. If I was going to do that, I'd do it somewhere closer to a cliff, make it easier to get rid of the body parts."

"That makes me feel so much better since I see you've thought this through."

He winked at her. "Ready to find one?"

She nodded.

They walked through the trees. The scent of pine and damp wood filled her nose. Gabrielle spotted a beautiful evergreen tree and ran to it almost falling several times.

"What about this one?"

Theo joined her and looked at the small, squat tree.

"That's a great tree... for a city apartment."

Gabrielle studied it. "You're probably right. It would be perfect for my living room. But I doubt anyone would even notice it in the lodge."

She spotted a large tree with thick wide branches and walked to it. "What about this one?"

Theo sized up the tree. He walked around it looking at the needles.

"Not too tall. Nice width. The needles look healthy. There aren't any bare spots. Can you hold this for a second?" He handed her the axe and then dug into the tree looking close inside it.

"What are you looking for?"

"Ladybugs."

"Ladybugs?" she asked incredulously.

He pulled his head out of the needles. "Our first Christmas at the lodge my dad and I went out and found a tree. It was like this one. We chopped it down.

Put it on the snowmobile. Brought it back to the lodge. Decorated it. And the next morning when we woke up there were ladybugs all over the lobby. They'd been nesting in there and woke up because of the warmth."

"You're joking."

He shook his head. "My sister still has nightmares."

Gabrielle laughed. "I think ladybugs are beautiful. Every spring my dad and I release them into his garden."

"I agree. But they are a bit less beautiful when you are picking them out of your hair, your toothbrush and your cereal for six months."

"Wait," said Gabrielle. "A snowmobile? We could have brought a snowmobile?"

Theo smiled. "I thought you wanted to get a better feel for the place. That's hard to do when you are rushing past at thirty miles an hour."

She nodded. "True."

"Plus I didn't picture you as one of those girls who hated to get some exercise."

"I'm not," she protested. "I just..." Flustered she couldn't think of an answer.

Theo laughed. "I'm kidding. Totally kidding. Though you do look adorable when you're flustered."

Gabrielle's cheeks warmed and Theo held his hand out for the axe.

"What? Do you think I can't chop down a tree?"

He held up his hands and retreated a step. "All right city girl. Let's see what you got."

Gabrielle walked to the tree and looked it over. She rounded it and contemplated where to cut. It was about a good eight to ten inches thick. She knew she needed to chop it toward the bottom, but wasn't sure exactly where. Hell, she'd never even swung an axe before. They could be there all day if she didn't figure it out quick.

"You have no idea what you are doing do you?"

"None whatsoever."

They laughed and she held the axe out to him.

"No city girl. I'm going to teach you how to chop down your first tree."

"All right then."

"Never know when you might be stuck in the mountains alone and need to chop down a tree."

"To make a house with?"

"Or just a fire."

Gabrielle snorted as Theo pointed out the spot where she needed to hit the tree. Then standing behind her he wrapped his arms around her and showed her how to hold the axe. A thrill shivered through her at the feel of his solid body wrapped around hers. She fought the urges that trickled through her mind as she tried to concentrate on what he showed her to do, but it wasn't easy.

Knock it off. He's just being nice. He's our assistant, remember?

Chapter Seven

Theo and his dad struggled to carry the enormous tree into the lodge front room as Gabrielle followed with his mom. He hadn't wanted to show weakness by telling her how heavy the tree was, but it was by far the largest tree he'd ever had to fell or carry into the lodge.

"Put it over there," said his mom.

"You mean the spot where we've put it for the last twenty years?" his father chided.

Theo and his dad dragged the tree in the corner and he heaved a sigh as he dropped the monster.

His mom set the stand down and held it in place. "Wow. I think the trunk will barely fit inside the stand this year."

"I believe it," Theo muttered.

"All right you two, let's see those muscles put to work."

Theo and his dad exchanged a look before each grabbing an end of the tree and trying to get it upright. The tree stand slipped and Gabrielle jumped in and helped steady the tree as it raised inch by inch.

"Perfect," his mom announced as the tree slid into place. She and Gabrielle screwed in the bolts as Theo wiped his face. Her rear hung in the air as she dove under the tree working right alongside his mom. For a moment he tried to imagine any of the girls he'd dated in the past three years getting down on their hands and knees to help without being asked. He couldn't see any of them doing any such thing- once again solidifying that he was doing the right thing by letting go of that life.

He didn't want a beautiful woman to show off in public anymore for the status it brought him. He wanted a down to earth woman whose beauty wasn't only external. Someone to share a life with. A life with kids and pets and school and church and soccer and volunteering. A life like the one he'd been raised in. He had no idea why it had taken him so long to realize that what his parents had was exactly what he wanted. He'd wasted so many years being envious of people who had stuff. When what he should have realized was that the only 'stuff' he needed had been there all along.

Gabrielle and his mom crawled out from under the tree and his mom stepped back inspecting it.

"Perfect," she announced with a smile.

Theo, Gabrielle and his dad join her.

"It's looking a little bare right now," said his dad.

"Then let's get the ornaments from the basement."

His parents walked out as Theo bumped Gabrielle's shoulder.

"Good pick.

"I'm just glad you looked for ladybugs. I would never have even thought of that."

"It would be quite an interesting Christmas, that's for sure. Especially for your client's special date."

She snorted. "I think any kind of bug would send her running straight to the nearest decontamination zone."

Theo reached up and picked several pine needles from Gabrielle's soft blonde hair.

She brushed dirt from her hands. "Man, I could really use a shower."

"Nah, you look great."

She looked up at him and arched an eyebrow.

He shoved his hands in his pockets. "What I mean is, you look... natural."

She eyed him. "Is that a nice way of saying I need to fix my makeup?"

"What? No. That's not what I meant at all. I mean, I..." What did he mean? "I just meant... you're pretty without makeup. You..."

She laughed. "I'm teasing. Breathe."

He chuckled. "Man. It's so hard to know what to say anymore. You say a girl looks nice and you're hitting on her. You say she looks natural, they think you're saying they need makeup. I can never seem to get it right."

"Well, I'm not like that. What you see is what you get with me. I don't have a hidden agenda or anything."

Gabrielle looked around the room and her gaze lit on the Wentworths sitting at a table. Her reading a book. Him reading the paper. She watched them for a moment, her brow creasing.

"Aren't those the people you helped in earlier?"

"Yup. Usual spots. Usual pastime."

Her expression fell. "That's so sad. They seemed so excited when they arrived."

"What's sad?"

"That they sit there not paying attention to each other in such an amazing place. Each in their own world. Doing something completely separate."

Theo stared at the Wentworths. He'd never really

thought about it before. They'd been coming to the lodge for as long as he could remember. Always doing the same thing every time. Him with his paper and coffee. Her with a book and tea.

"Yeah, I guess it is kind of. But when you've been married as long as they have, I guess it's bound to happen."

Her jaw dropped open. "That's even sadder that you think that."

Theo's parents entered with several boxes of ornaments and decorations.

"Found them!" his mom announced. "Though the tree is so big this year, I'm not sure we'll have enough to fill the whole thing."

"We could start with just the part people will see," offered Gabrielle.

His mom nodded and together the women dug into the ornament boxes, pulling them out one by one and talking about them.

He supposed Gabrielle was right. When he'd been married for as long as the Wentworths were he hoped that he and his wife would still be doing things together, not just in the same room.

.   .   .

Theo was up on a ladder hanging ornaments where his mom told him. Gabrielle pulled out ornaments and handed them to Ronald.

Theo's mom stared at the tree. "To the right. No to the left. No higher. No-"

His dad shook his head. "Just put it on the tree, son."

Gabrielle laughed.

"If we put too many clumped together it will look lopsided," said his mom.

"They aren't clumped together," replied his dad.

"Yes, they are."

Theo's dad kissed her head. "It looks perfect like always." He led her away. "Come on. Let's go see if we can find the star to go on top while Theo and Gabrielle finish up."

"But-"

Theo came down the ladder and helped Gabrielle with the last few ornaments.

"They're super cute," she said.

"That's one word for it."

As they finished hanging the ornaments Gabrielle looked over her shoulder.

"They're still sitting there," she whispered. "I don't think they've even spoken to each other the whole time we've been in here."

Theo looked at the Wentworths. "It's really bugging you isn't?"

"I guess I just think, what if that's what ends up happening to the couples I help. That would make me so sad."

"What do you suggest?"

Gabrielle's face scrunched up. "Do you have any board games?"

Theo hitched his thumb over his shoulder. "We have some in the supply closet."

Gabrielle burst into a large grin. "Show me."

THEO TURNED ON THE LIGHT TO A CLOSET filled with shelves of old decorations from his mom's different decorating phases as well as art supplies, and other odds and ends.

"They're up there." He pointed.

Gabrielle walked into the closet and looked around. "What is all this stuff?"

"Leftovers from parties and celebrations. Decorations from my mom's Christmas in July phase. Her Mardi Gras for Cinco de Mayo phase. And of course, her Merry Christmakkah phase."

Gabrielle chuckled and bent down pulling out

several canvases and easels as well as paint supplies. "Did you have a paint party?"

"Mom's an artist."

Gabrielle stared at the supplies for a moment before putting them back. "Good to know."

She stood and looked over at the shelf with games. She rifled through them for a moment and grabbed Monopoly, showing it to him.

"I have the best idea." Her eyes sparkled with mischief.

※ ❄ ❀

GABRIELLE AND THEO WALKED BACK INTO THE main room. She spotted Ronald putting the star on the tree under Margery's supervision. Margery waved as they passed and Gabrielle approached the Wentworths.

"Mr. and Mrs. Wentworth? I'd like to introduce you to my new friend Gabrielle Miller," said Theo.

Mrs. Wentworth put her book in her lap and took off her glasses. "Nice to meet you, Gabrielle."

Gabrielle shook the game. "We were just going to play Monopoly and I wondered if maybe you'd like to play with us."

The Wentworths look at each other.

"Oh, I haven't played games in ages," said Mrs. Wentworth.

"That's because you got tired of losing," her husband chided.

Mrs. Wentworth closed her book and let her gaze fall heavily on him. "Are you saying you are better than me at Monopoly?"

A handsome crooked smile creased his features. "Well... I do dabble in real estate."

"All right Mr. Know-It-All. You're on."

Mr. Wentworth's smile fell a bit. "On for what?"

She set her book and glasses on the table next to her. "Playing Monopoly."

Gabrielle smiled. "How about we make a wager."

The Wentworths looked at Gabrielle.

"Theo and I against the two of you. If you win, we have to cook you dinner tomorrow."

"And if you win?" asked Mr. Wentworth.

"Neither of us cook," Mrs. Wentworth added.

Gabrielle thought for a minute. She could kill two birds with one stone while being stuck at the lodge. She could find out the best thing to do for Chantel's date and help the Wentworths in the process. At least that was the plan she'd come up with in the closet. And it was perfect. Then she could take a couple who obviously needed a little rekindling and help them bring back the spark while trying to figure out Chantel's date. Plus, it would give her people to do something with if Theo had other things to do.

"If we win... You have to spend tomorrow with us doing whatever we want."

"You're on," said Mrs. Wentworth.

Gabrielle smiled. She could pretty much hug herself for getting them to agree.

Chapter Eight

The group sat at a table neck-deep in their game. Hotels and houses filled the Monopoly board. Drinks and a mostly eaten bowl of popcorn sat between them. Daniel silently prayed over his dice before throwing them.

"Praying will do you no good Mr. Wentworth. You land on any of those next six properties and we win." Theo winked at Gabrielle. He hadn't thought much of playing with the Wentworths but they were surprisingly fun and Gabrielle kept the banter both witty and light, which helped them come out of their shells more than he'd ever seen. Gabrielle was infectious. When she smiled he found himself smiling. When she laughed, other people laughed too. Her entire presence lit the room brighter than the huge Christmas tree in the corner.

Daniel looked at Jennifer. "Blow on them for luck?"

She eyed him skeptically and then smiled before blowing on the dice. He threw them on the board.

Gabrielle cheered and high fived Theo.

"Wahoo! That's you on Park Place with the hotels you owe me three thousand and fifty dollars."

Daniel clutched his heart and Jennifer chuckled and patted him on the back. "Maybe we should have played more."

"Who knew I'd be so bad at a real estate game?"

Gabrielle began gathering up the pieces on the board. "We won so now you have to spend the day with us tomorrow."

"And what do you propose we do all day?" asked Daniel.

"Does it matter?" asked Jennifer. "Anything has to be better than sitting and reading a paper all day."

Daniel smiled. "Well it's a good thing you read book instead then, isn't it."

Gabrielle said, "I don't know what we're going to do yet but how about meet here tomorrow at nine a.m. and I'll have a plan."

Daniel stood and extended his hand to Gabrielle.

"You beat me at Monopoly. I think you've both earned the right to call me Daniel."

Gabrielle shook his hand.

"And please, call me Jennifer," said Jennifer.

Daniel looked at Jennifer and held his hand out to her. "Well, my dear. I'm ready to retire. You coming?"

Jennifer looked at his out stretched hand and a smile broke across her face as she looked to Gabrielle and Theo and then back to Daniel. She placed her hand in his and the two walked out of the room.

Theo shook his head. "Wow."

"What?" Gabrielle asked.

Theo picked up the money off the board and put it in the box. "You really are a magic worker. I've never seen them touch before."

Gabrielle shrugged. "Well, then we're off to a good start."

Theo stared at her for a moment while she continued to clear off the board. It amazed him to see a girl want to help others without wanting anything in return. The girls he'd dated in the past years were nothing like Gabrielle. Once again reaffirming to him that he really needed to change his life.

"So? What's on the agenda for tomorrow?"

She glanced at him sideways and smiled. "I have a few ideas." Her smile fell and her eyes widened. "Oh my gosh! I didn't even think to ask you if you were busy tomorrow. I'm so sorry. You aren't busy are you? It's just... you seem to like the outdoors and stuff and my client likes the outdoors so you're kind of perfect to help me put this date together."

He'd rarely seen someone throw themselves into their job and take it as seriously as she did. "This date means a lot to you, doesn't it?"

"To be honest my business is my heart and right now my heart is failing. If I get this one date right, it could change everything for me. Not just because of the money but because of the advertising it could bring in as well."

Theo sighed. "That's amazing. It's too bad then I can't help you with it. I actually have a pretty full day."

She stopped and looked up at him. "You do?"

Theo crossed his arms over his chest and hid the smile that threatened to peek through. "It's my shoes."

Her eyebrows drew together. "Your shoes?"

He nodded. "They've been begging me to polish them for like, a year now." He couldn't help but smile as her eyes crinkled and she shook her head.

"Uh-huh."

"And my shirts are in a pretty serious need of ironing."

She nodded. "Of course."

"And then there's my email I need to clean out and my receipts I need to organize and-"

Gabrielle snorted before grabbing the game and putting the lid on.

"I'm serious. I am busy. Super busy. So much stuff to do."

She smiled. "I can tell."

"I may be busy all day."

Gabrielle looked at him for a moment before walking toward the doorway. "Well, if your shoes decide they can wait to be polished, I'll be here at nine a.m. with Daniel and Jennifer."

"I'll talk to them tonight. They're tough negotiators but I might be able to persuade them if I threaten to take them out in the snow, without waterproofing them first."

Gabrielle laughed and looked back at him. "Nite."

Theo waved. "Nite."

He watched her go as his mom entered from the opposite direction.

"She seems sweet."

Theo rolled his eyes. *Oh no, here it comes.* 'She does," he finally said.

His mom picked up the popcorn bowl and glasses. "Pretty too."

He wasn't ready to have another conversation

about girls with his mom. She'd made her wishes for him to settle down known for the last five years. She'd also been very vocal about her dislike of the girls he'd dated. Whatever he said now could get him in deeper with his mom, or stop her in her tracks.

"I hadn't noticed," he lied.

His mom cocked an eyebrow at him. "I'm sure of that."

Together they cleaned up the rest of the table. Theo waited for the other shoe to drop. He knew his mom too well to know that she always had more to say.

"Have you... officially ended things with Miss Instafamous?"

Ahhhhh... there it was. That other huge, colorful, clown shoe. He'd rather go back to talking about Gabrielle. "Her name is Chantel."

"Oh, that's right."

Theo groaned inwardly. "I tried to call her yesterday but her phone dropped."

She stopped cleaning and the gaze only a mother could give dropped on him and demanded his attention. Theo blew out a harsh breath.

"Look, she has to already knows it's over. I told her we needed to separate. I haven't returned her calls in weeks and we haven't even seen each other in over a month and a half."

His mom's lips pursed together. "Okay. If you say so. I just don't want to see you or Gabrielle get hurt."

"Mom. Gabrielle and I just had some food and played a game together. It's not like we're getting married."

"All I'm saying is you need to make sure it's over for good before you start anything with someone as nice as Gabrielle. I would hate for either of you to get hurt by a simple miscommunication." She kissed Theo's cheek and then hugged him. "I can't tell you how proud I am of you."

Theo snorted.

"I'm serious. I was really worried about you for a while. All those parties and fancy cars and suits that cost more than my entire wardrobe. It wasn't you."

"It took me a while to figure that out."

"But you did and that's what is important." She headed toward the kitchen but then stopped at the door and turned back. "Just out of curiosity, Gabrielle doesn't like aromatherapy candles, does she?"

"Ha-ha. Very funny." His smile dropped and he gave his most serious expression. "At least I don't think so. Do you think I should go find out?"

Margery shook her head and laughed.

Gabrielle walked into her room, looked around and then lifted the phone receiver.

"Patty? Hi, it's Gabrielle. There wasn't a suitcase delivered for me today was there?"

"Sorry. No delivery, hun."

"Okay. Thanks."

Gabrielle hung up the phone, pulled out her cell and texted Evie.

Gabrielle: *Where's my bag?*

Evie: *Oh my gosh! I totally forgot! I am so sorry. Seriously?*

"Great. Just great."

The following morning Daniel and Jennifer were already waiting in the lodge front room when Theo walked down to see them talking to his mom.

"Good morning," said his mom.

"Hello," replied Jennifer setting down her book.

"What do you two have planned for the day?"

Daniel shook his paper as he turned the page. "We

don't know. Theo and Gabrielle beat us at Monopoly and now we are at their disposal all day long."

"Really?"

Theo continued to the front desk where Patty held out the mail to him and he looked through it before handing it back to her. Gabrielle walked toward him wearing the same clothes as the day before. Her makeup had been removed and her hair looked not quite as well groomed as the day before.

"Morning."

She smiled and tucked her hair behind her ear. How's the shoe shining going?"

"Well, I had a long talk with them and reminded them that they are snow boots and those don't actually need polishing. They weren't happy but in the end they agreed."

"How very diplomatic of you."

"Not to be rude but, aren't those the clothes you wore yesterday?"

She groaned. "My bag didn't come yesterday. I was going to see if it made it here this morning."

"No way," said Patty. "The pass was snowed in last night in the storm. There won't be anyone getting in or out for at least seventy-two hours."

Gabrielle's eyes popped wide. "No. That's not

possible. I have a client coming in and I'm supposed to be out of here by Sunday."

"When is the Santa and elf duet?" asked Theo

"Christmas Eve."

"Well, that's a week away you have plenty of time."

A frantic note tinged her voice. "Yes, but I have to get home and help wrap all the presents. My mom makes several hundred cookies and baked goods..."

Theo rested his hands on her arms. "It's okay. Breathe. You're gonna get there in time if I have to snowmobile you down the mountain myself, all right?"

She nodded and blew out a breath.

"In the meantime, I know my sister left some clothes and stuff here in her room. Why don't I go find you something to change into and some toiletries, then we can go meet Daniel and Jennifer."

She looked at him conflicted. To his surprise he found that the possibility of not spending the day with her bummed him out more than he had anticipated.

"Thank you." She threw him a tight smile.

Theo squeezed her arm and ran toward the stairs. He needed to hurry. He didn't want her changing her mind.

Gabrielle checked her phone.

Gabrielle: *Snowed in. May be a couple days before you can get through.*

Evie: *Dang it. Okay. I'll let her highness know. Sorry again about your bag.*

Gabrielle's fingers hovered over the keys and then she shoved her phone in her pocket.

Theo jogged back down the stairs toward her with an armful of clothes, a toothbrush and toothpaste still in the packaging and a hair brush.

"I'm not sure they will fit you but I got some stuff that should keep you warm at least. There's a pair of pajamas in there too." He held them out to her.

She looked over the pile. They looked worn but not too bad. "Are you sure she won't mind?"

"I'm sure."

She looked at the pile again and nodded. "I'll be right back." She walked back toward her room and couldn't help but notice Patty watching them from behind the desk with a schoolgirl smile on her face.

Theo talked to Jennifer and Daniel as Gabrielle entered feeling as stupid as a girl wearing a paper bag to the prom. The clothes Theo had handed her looked like they'd been made in the nineties and for someone a few good pounds larger than she was. She'd picked out the best of the holiday sweatshirts- a bright green number with a sequin tree on it- and a pair of red leggings sporting Christmas presents and kittens.

Theo spotted her and stifled a laugh.

"Oh my." Jennifer covered the smile that spread over her face.

"You look... colorful." Daniel nodded.

"Did I forget to mention that my sister left them here because she lost some weight?" asked Theo.

Gabrielle planted her hands on her hips and looked down at herself. "I think you did forget to mention that. And that she was obsessed with Christmas?"

"You look lovely," Jennifer offered. "Very festive."

Festive was one word for it. "Thank you." Gabrielle knew Jennifer was just being nice, but she appreciated the gesture nonetheless.

"So. What are we doing today?" asked Daniel.

"I thought we'd start with making breakfast. The chef said he's willing to give us all a cooking lesson. He's gonna teach us to make a cheese soufflé." Gabrielle pulled on the edge of her sweatshirt.

"I love soufflé!" Jennifer smiled.

Daniel threw Theo a dubious expression and Theo threw up his hands.

"This is all her.," he said. "I didn't make the plans."

Jennifer got to her feet. "Come on you old grump. Let's learn to make a soufflé. Then you can make them for me when we get home."

Daniel snorted. "Yeah right."

Jennifer pulled him to his feet and the group headed toward the kitchen.

"Soufflé?" Theo questioned. "Isn't that a little above our beginner pay grade?"

Gabrielle shrugged. "I've always wanted to try a soufflé. They sound so exotic."

"And very difficult to make."

"How do we know unless we try?"

Theo smiled down on her and warmth heated her skin, making her wish she hadn't chosen to wear a sweatshirt.

THE GROUP OF FOUR STOOD AT THE COUNTER wearing red and green aprons, and chef hats. Their ingredients have been laid out in front of them meticulously by the straight-spined, eagle-eyed chef who paced back and forth in front of them like an Army General.

"There will be no hanky-panky in my kitchen. Do you understand? We are here for me to teach you how to make a soufflé. Soufflés are not just like cooking scrambled eggs. They take skill. Precision. And talent. Something which I am sure all of you lack."

Daniel huffed. "Now wait-"

"SILENCE!" ordered the chef. "This is my kitchen. You will do as I say. Or you will not do! Do we understand each other Mr. CEO?"

Daniel frowned and began to take off his apron.

Gabrielle's heart pounded. Maybe this wasn't the best idea...

"Oh, come on now Daniel, we made a wager." Jennifer laid a gentle hand on Daniel's arm.

He stopped and looked at her and for a fraction of a second Gabrielle thought he might leave despite his wife's plea. But then Daniel mumbled something and put his apron back on. Jennifer smiled and patted his cheek.

"It's been a long time since you've had to take orders from someone else."

"Let us begin." The chef smacked the counter with a spatula, making Theo jump. The chef looked at Gabrielle and winked and smiled before turning his back on the group.

OVER THE NEXT FORTY MINUTES THE CHEF instructed them on how to crack their eggs, fold them together, the order to mix in ingredients, and how to pour the contents into little cups. Theo bumped Gabrielle as she poured the batter, making her spill.

"Miss Miller really, if you can't even pour batter what are you doing in my kitchen?"

Theo snickered and Gabrielle glared at him. Though they all had fun making the soufflés she doubted that Chantel would want to do any cooking in the kitchen with Chef Meticuloso.

After cleaning up their messes and sterilizing the counter tops twice, the bell rang on the oven and they all crowded around as the chef pulled out their creations.

Jennifer, Gabrielle, and Daniel cheered at the sight of their fluffy soufflés.

"Maybe next time you shouldn't whip them so hard," Gabrielle said, looking at Theo's deflated pancake.

"Oh really? You think I whipped the eggs too hard?"

She shrugged. "Possibly, or you could just be terrible at baking."

"Ha. Ha," said Theo. "I'll have you know I make a mean English muffin."

Gabrielle laughed. "Really?"

"Yes. And I pour orange juice into a glass well too."

"You're just full of surprises."

The chef set the soufflés on the counter and inspected them. As if on cue Gabrielle's soufflé wilted under his scrutiny. Theo chuckled and Gabrielle threw flour in his face. Surprised, he threw some back but got it all in her hair.

"I'm sorry. I'm so sorry." He wiped at her face as she spit flour onto his shirt.

"Hey!" said the chef. "No horsing around in here."

"Yes, Chef," she and Theo said together.

The group inspected Daniel and Jennifer's soufflés as Gabrielle continued to blow flour off her face.

"We did it!" said Jennifer. "We really did it!" Just as she finished speaking, her soufflé popped like a balloon.

Daniel cheered. "I won. I won." He claps and then regained his composure. "I knew I'd win."

Everyone held up their terrible soufflés as the chef snapped a photo of them all, and then handed the phone to Theo. Theo turned the phone so she could see the photo.

Gabrielle laughed in horror as her hair sticks out all over and her face is still smudged with flour. "Oh my gosh, delete that. Delete it right now."

"No way." Theo shoved the phone in his pocket. "I

think I'm going to frame that one and put it out in the restaurant."

Gabrielle picked flour from her hair and threw it at him. "You better not."

"A big eighteen inch by twenty-four inch print. We can hang it near the entrance."

Theo laughed and Gabrielle looked over at Daniel and Jennifer who were eating each other's soufflés. Jennifer looked to Gabrielle and winked.

Gabrielle nudged Theo. He looked at the couple and then at her.

"That's why I do what I do," she whispered.

THE GROUP WALKED TO THE FRONT OF THE lodge.

"So, what's next that I can win at?" asked Daniel.

Jennifer playfully slapped Daniel's shoulder and he chuckled before offering her his arm.

Theo watched them, surprised with how much they'd transformed in such a short amount of time. And then a pang of jealousy wormed through him at their affection and he wished selfishly that Gabrielle wasn't so fixed on helping the Wentworths. For the first time in a long time, he wanted to be alone with someone.

Gabrielle's easy air and fun personality were just what Theo had been searching for. Someone who knew how to let loose and be themselves. Someone who could wear clothes a dozen sizes too big and not even worry what they looked like or what someone else might think. Someone who cared more about helping other people than about her own comfort. He'd never met anyone like her before. Theo wondered if it could all be an act. If she was just putting on a performance. Theo figured if Gabrielle wanted to be an actress she could be, but he doubted that even she had the talent to fool everyone around her into thinking she was that kind if she wasn't.

"Everyone should get on some warm clothes because we're gonna head outside," Gabrielle announced.

The Wentworths disappeared down the hallway and Theo stared at Gabrielle. Could she really be as amazing as she seemed?

She looked up at him. "I think I need to wash up and see if any more of your sister's hand me downs will work for outside."

"I'll go grab my coat and boots."

"The boots you didn't polish? Are you sure they'll cooperate?" she teased.

"Yes, but only because I will be taking them outside. They get offended when I just use them to walk around the lodge."

She snickered and started toward her room.

He wanted to say something to her. Something witty that would make her smile again, but before he could think of anything his phone rang.

He pulled it from his pocket and looked at it.

Chantel? His finger hovered over the call button for a moment and then he hit the end button instead, sending it to voicemail. What the heck? After the conversation he'd just had with his mom all of a sudden she called him? He didn't even know how to respond. Why would she be calling him after all the time apart? He probably needed to find out, but he didn't want to do anything that might dampen his budding happy mood at the moment.

Chapter Nine

Theo and Gabrielle were on a snowmobile with Daniel and Jennifer behind them, riding through the snow. Theo stopped his snowmobile and Daniel and Jennifer pulled up beside them.

"I have never been snow-mobiling before. This is so much fun," said Gabrielle

"The last time we went was in Yellowstone National Park. They told us that it would take two hours to get to Old Faithful. Four hours later we finally made it. Missed the eruption by ten minutes, turned around and came back. We couldn't walk for days," replied Jennifer.

"There were some good things about that trip. I got to sit with your arms around me for eight hours."

Jennifer smiled at Daniel. "Remember Willis? He wanted a photo of that buffalo."

Daniel groaned. "Instead, he got his snowmobile buried in a three-foot snow bank and we had to dig him out."

"Sounds like you two used to have lots of fun together." The thought made Gabrielle smile.

Daniel squeezed Jennifer's hand. "We sure did. Before we got old."

"Before you got old," Jennifer retorted.

His eyebrows drew together. "You're the one who started reading books all the time."

"Because you started working around the clock."

"Only because-"

"How about we go a little bit further and then we can stop?" Theo offered.

"I packed some food and a blanket," Gabrielle offered.

Jennifer chuckled. "That sounds lovely."

Gabrielle looked at Theo and he nodded. They took off again and she wrapped her arms around his waist enjoying the feel of his hard torso more than she should have.

. . .

THEO SET UP THE BLANKET AS GABRIELLE pulled out a couple thermoses and some sandwiches the chef had prepared.

Both couples sat and sipped cocoa in silence for a moment. She wanted to see Jennifer and Daniel get along again. She wanted to relight that spark that had drawn them together.

"So, tell us, how did you two meet?" she asked.

Jennifer and Daniel looked at each other and both laughed. "We were in college and my roommate and I both had blind dates on the same night. Daniel showed up and I went with him. It wasn't until later that we found out he was meant to go with my roommate," said Jennifer.

"Which I was very glad I didn't. You were much prettier." Daniel kissed her cheek. "Still are."

Jennifer smiled. "I was glad to get you too. You were much taller than my date."

They all laughed. Daniel looked deeply at Jennifer and pushed a hair from her face. She smiled and kissed his hand. Gabrielle nudged Theo as her heart squeezed.

Theo's eyes widened and he mouthed, *Wow!*

It was working. The thought warmed her and sent her mind whirling. This could open up a whole new division of her company. Helping couples not only get together, but stay together. Helping couples rekindle things that might have gotten put on the back burner while raising a family.

"How did you two meet?" Daniel finally asked them.

Gabrielle looked at Theo and then back to Daniel. "Us? Oh, we just met yesterday."

"Yesterday?"

"That's so hard to believe," said Jennifer. "The way you two act I would have thought you'd been a couple for years."

"I'm meeting a client." Gabrielle's cheeks heated and she sipped her hot cocoa refusing to meet Theo's eye.

"Gabrielle is at the lodge for business," Theo offered.

It was true. Things between them were easier than it had ever been with a guy before. Theo wasn't just good looking; he was a good guy. Fun, kind, and family oriented. The kind of guy she would be definitely be interested in... if she was looking for a guy- which she totally wasn't.

"What kind of work do you do?" Daniel asked.

"Consulting."

"Good for you. Make your own hours. Be your own boss."

"Exactly. I love what I do and I can't see doing

anything else with my life. Though being my own boss can be stressful at times."

"Owning your own business always is. But the benefits are definitely worth it."

"Theo, have you made the switch to working at the lodge full time?" asked Jennifer.

"I'd like to but we'd need the lodge to do a lot more year-round business for me to be able to."

"Still having trouble getting spring and summer business?" asked Daniel.

Theo nodded.

"That's so strange," said Gabrielle. "I'd have thought summer camps and stuff would have been great business for you."

Theo shrugged. "Mom and dad don't have the energy to chase dozens of kids around all summer anymore and I doubt Patty would be interested either. And it's not like they can afford to take on any new hires unless they got a loan. But I doubt anyone would loan them money on the old lodge. It's kind of one of those round robin problems."

Gabrielle's chest squeezed. Though Theo wasn't saying it, she could tell the lodge was in trouble. She just wished there was something she could do to help.

Everyone looked out at the view.

"I can see why you'd want to live here, Theo. It's

beautiful. I could stay forever," Gabrielle said without thinking. Why the heck did she keep thinking and saying such silly things? She really needed to get it together before he thought she was nothing more than a giddy schoolgirl vying for his attention.

THREE HOURS LATER THEO, GABRIELLE, Daniel and Jennifer walked through the front door of the lodge.

"We should lose to you at Monopoly more often. Today was a lot of fun," said Jennifer.

"Then we should continue it tomorrow," Gabrielle offered. "I am sure there are still several things we could do that Theo hasn't shown me yet."

Daniel looked at Jennifer and shrugged. "Where and when Boss?"

Gabrielle held her breath for a moment. Please let Jennifer say yes.

"Why not?" Jennifer answered.

Gabrielle fought the urge to fist pump the air.

"Shall we say ten a.m.?" Theo said.

Daniel and Jennifer nodded, took hands and walk off.

"So, you up for another adventure tomorrow?"

Gabrielle asked. "I understand if you have other things you need to do."

Theo crossed his bulky arms over is chest. "What do you have in mind?"

"I'm not entirely sure. Anything you suggest we do?"

"Well, we've cut down a tree. We've gone snow-mobiling-"

"Which we could have done to get the tree."

"True but that wouldn't have been as fun as watching you try and help drag the tree back."

"I did help," she protested.

He smiled. "Of course you did."

She gave him a mock offended glare.

"There's sledding. We could go into town and go shopping. Uh... there's a ballroom-"

"A ballroom?"

"Yeah, it has a stage and everything."

Her mind flew into a flurry of ideas.

"What are you thinking?" he asked, narrowing his eyes.

She smiled and pressed her lips together. "I'm not telling."

"All right, keep your secrets."

They stared at each other for a moment. She wanted to say something. It surprised her that even though they'd had a long morning and afternoon she had no desire to go back to her room and be alone. But it wasn't just being alone. She wanted more time with Theo. But unable to think of anything else to say to keep the conversation going she waved and started off.

"Then I'll see you tomorrow."

"Okay see ya."

Gabrielle got a few feet away and looked over her shoulder to where he stood, watching her go. "Bye."

He waved. "Bye."

She turned around and continued to the hallway for her room. She wanted to see if he still watched her, but she didn't want to make things more awkward than she already had. If he'd wanted her to stay and spend more time with him he would have asked her, wouldn't he?

THEO WATCHED GABRIELLE WALK AWAY IN the ridiculous clothes he'd given to her and couldn't help but smile inwardly. She'd not once complained, or checked her phone to see if she had any new messages or to update her status on social media or anything.

Yes, Gabrielle was beautiful, but it was more than that. It went deeper. She was... unique. Like a unicorn.

What? Had he really just thought of her like a unicorn? Was he losing his mind? A unicorn. Ridiculous. But in all honesty, she kind of was like a unicorn. He'd never met a girl like her before. Selfless and kind, he'd watched her light up every time the Wentworths had touched or laughed or joked with each other. As if her happiness only came from their happiness.

He continued to watch her until she was out of sight and then the hairs on his neck prickled and he looked over to see his mom and Patty staring at him with wide grins on their faces.

"It's only six," said his mom. "Why don't you invite her to dinner?"

As much as he wanted to do just that, he didn't want to give his mom and Patty any encouragement in their suggestions for his love life.

"Thanks but I'm good."

Theo turned and headed up the stairs to his room. Dark thoughts shrouded him. What was he missing? What did she hide? No one was that nice. He'd learned that first hand. No one was as picture perfect as the photos they posted on social media. Somewhere hidden behind the façade was pain, or loss, or anger, or jealousy or... something.

Theo blew out a breath and ran his hands through his hair. Man. He really was jaded. It was just that kind of thinking that had him doing anything he could to get out of the city and back to the mountains where he belonged. Back to his roots. Back to what really mattered.

He shook his head and walked down the hallway. Why couldn't Gabrielle genuinely be as nice as she seemed? Maybe he was being so critical to try and save himself from being hurt. Because deep inside he feared that if she knew the kind of playboy he'd been until recently, she'd run straight back for the city and vanish from his life forever. And even though it had only been two days, he was pretty sure that he'd never find another girl like her again.

Chapter Ten

The following morning Gabrielle, Theo, Daniel and Jennifer sat in the middle of the ballroom in front of easels with large canvases sitting on them. Theo's mom stood near the stage with an easel of her own showing them how to paint. Theo wasn't sure how or when she'd gotten his parents to agree to help out but she must have worked a miracle to get his dad to dress like Santa and sit in a chair next to a Christmas tree on the stage. His dad liked to have fun, but he didn't like looking stupid, especially in front of guests. What Gabrielle had done to earn such favor with his dad, he had no idea.

Cheery Christmas music played in the background as each of them tried to paint the portrait. Theo had pretty much given up as soon as they'd started, but he enjoyed sitting with the others, critiquing Gabrielle's painting skills and messing with his dad. He grabbed a cookie off Gabrielle's plate and took a bite.

"Hey, that was mine," she chided.

"Mine are all gone."

"Because you ate them. And mine will be all gone too in a minute if you don't stop eating them."

He threw her his best smile and winked at her. "I have a friend in the kitchen. He'll hook us up with some more if you want."

"Have a mentioned how stupid I feel?" his father interrupted.

"Many times," Theo replied.

"Does it mean I can stop now?"

"No!" Everyone shouted at the same time.

They broke into laughter. His dad snuck a cookie from the table next to him and grumbled.

"Stop that!" said his mom. "You're getting crumbs in your beard. And we are losing continuity if you eat the cookies."

"I'm hungry. I've been sitting here for hours."

"We're almost done. I'm pretty sure you won't starve to death for not eating for two hours."

Gabrielle smiled. "Your parents are so great."

Theo looked over and his mom wiped crumbs from his dad's fake beard and then kissed his cheek.

He couldn't help but smile. His parents' relationship had always been full of fun and adventure. It hadn't always been roses and rarely had ever been champagne, but through it all they'd stuck together and continued to work at it.

"Yeah, they are pretty great."

"They remind me of my parents."

"Really?"

She nodded. "My parents are the reason I got into the business I'm in. They've been married for over thirty years. I've never seen another couple so happy to be together. I wanted to help create that for other people. Help them to find their perfect partner in crime to adventure through the years with."

"I like that. Partners in crime. That does make life sound like an adventure."

"Life gets hard for everyone. My parents say that if you treat it like an adventure, it makes even the bad times more bearable."

"Your parents sound like great people. I'd love to meet them."

Gabrielle's cheeks flushed a delicate shade of pink and she pushed her hair from her eyes. "Well, maybe someday you can."

Was that an invitation? He was pretty sure she was being polite. But for some reason meeting her parents sounded like something he'd like to do. He'd never been much into meeting the families of the girls he dated before, but to raise someone like Gabrielle, they had to be great. Plus, he'd love to see her all dressed up in an elf outfit.

His mom walked by and looked at everyone's portraits.

"Nicely done Jenny, but Dan... You might want to stick to your day job."

Everyone chuckled, surprisingly including Daniel.

Theo had always thought of the Wentworths as nice but rather stuffy people. What surprised him most was that they kept coming to the lodge. He would have expected so see them sitting in a chalet in Switzerland enjoying the fire while being waited on hand and foot by a butler and maid rather than Hart's Lodge. But from everything he'd learned about them in the last day he realized how much he'd misjudged them.

He glanced at Gabrielle who chatted with Jennifer about their paintings. She hadn't misjudged them though. Not a bit. She'd known exactly what they needed. Theo stood and stretched. Gabrielle turned his way and smiled. Without thinking he reached out and brushed a paint smudge from her cheekbone. His fingers lingered for a moment on her soft skin as a thrill swept through him, and then he caught Jennifer smiling at him over Gabrielle's shoulder and he pulled away.

"Sorry you had a smudge."

Gabrielle reached up and wiped her cheek, her eyes never leaving his. "Thank you." Her voice came out husky and low, and for a moment he wished they were alone in a chateau in Switzerland snuggled up by a fire together.

Theo cleared his throat and pointed to her painting, trying to turn his thoughts away from the lips he wished he were kissing.

"So was this your test run for what you want to do for your client?"

Gabrielle set her brush down. "I'm not sure. I think the snowmobiling is great, but-" She leaned in and whispered. "To be honest I did the painting for them." She gestured toward Daniel and Jennifer.

"Might I suggest an idea?" he offered.

"Sure."

Theo held his hand out and winked at her. She took it and stood. He pulled her closer and the warmth of her fingers sent tingles through him. He leaned in and caught a whiff of the Lodge's shampoo on her hair.

"Play along," he whispered.

Her fingers squeezed his hand and again he wished

he could just lean in and kiss her. *Come on boy, back off!* He was pretty sure she might slap him if he tried.

"Daniel," he said, backing up a step. "I heard a rumor that you two used to ballroom dance for competitions."

Daniel raised an eyebrow and looked to Theo's parents and then back again. "I wonder where you heard that."

Theo's parents suddenly looked very deep in conversation when Daniel eyed them.

"Would you be interested in giving us a lesson?" Gabrielle asked

Daniel looked at Jennifer.

"It's been a while," she said.

"Just like riding a bike, right?"

"That's been even longer." She laughed.

Daniel held his hand out and Jennifer took it. Like royalty they glided out onto the floor while his mom hurried and changed the music.

"Does that mean I can I move now," his dad called.

"Yes," everyone said.

"Finally." His dad tugged off his Santa beard and stuffed a cookie in his mouth.

Gabrielle swallowed hard as Theo led her out onto the ballroom floor. She tried to drown the goldfish swimming in her stomach at his touch. She was there to do a job and he was just helping out. She didn't have time for his "help" to become anything more. She needed to stay focused and then once she'd done what Chantel wanted, she had to focus on her business even more.

With Chantel's recommendation it could literally explode overnight- but Gabrielle had a hard time denying the shiver that traversed her skin as Theo wrapped his arm around her waist and took her hand in his. Her body flushed with heat and she swallowed, trying not to let her nervousness show.

"I promise to try not to step on your toes," he said.

Gabrielle smiled and looked up at him. "And I'll try not to step on yours."

Theo chuckled. A deep rumbly sound that made her smile wider.

Knock it off you look like an idiot, she told herself.

They spent the next thirty minutes with Daniel and Jennifer trying to teach them the steps to the waltz. How to hold their hands and stand and move.

In the end she and Theo did pretty well- well, better than his parents who gave up after the first ten minutes. They succeeded in not stepping on each other's toes and even made it around the floor a few times without messing up. But when the Wentworths tried to teach them the fox trot- they were out. They moved to stand next to Theo's parents and soon a small crowd gathered to watch the Wentworths as they went from the fox trot to the cha-cha to the swing. If they hadn't told Gabrielle they hadn't danced in years she never would have believed it. They smiled and moved around the floor like they'd been practicing every day.

"They're amazing," said Gabrielle.

"I had no idea they could move like that," said Theo.

"If I'd known they were still that good I would have had them teaching classes years ago," replied Margery.

"That's a great idea," said Gabrielle. "Look how happy they are. I bet they would love to do it. You should ask them."

Margery winked at Gabrielle. "I think I'll talk to them about it after you two are done taking them out and showing them such a good time."

Gabrielle looked up at Theo and he smiled down

at her. As much as she didn't have time or the desire for romance, she was glad the she had Theo to do things with. And she liked that she could help Daniel and Jennifer.

The Wentworths stopped with the song and everyone clapped. Jennifer looked over as if noticing them all for the first time.

"Oh please," she said. "We were rusty as two robots from the Victorian age."

"You were wonderful, darling," said Daniel. "You carried me and my club feet as always." He kissed her hand and Jennifer blushed and waved him off.

The audience disappeared and the Wentworths approached. "Children, it has been a wonderful afternoon, but I have a few business things I need to attend to," said Daniel.

"And I think after such a workout I need to take a few minutes rest," said Jennifer. "Maybe tomorrow we could treat you two to lunch. Since you've done so much for us."

Theo and Gabrielle looked at each other and Theo shrugged.

"We all need to eat," he said.

"Great. We'll order our car and meet you in the lobby at noon," said Daniel.

Theo shook Daniel's hand. "Have a great evening."

Jennifer took both of Gabrielle's hands in hers and squeezed them. "I can't thank you enough," she whispered.

Daniel offered Jennifer his arm and they waved goodbye.

"I hope you didn't have any important plans for tomorrow. Like painting your nails and washing your hair or anything," said Theo.

"Well, you know..." Gabrielle chuckled. "Not at all. I like Daniel and Jennifer. I feel like we're really helping them to rekindle what they once had."

Theo cocked an eyebrow and a sexy smile caressed his face. "So, you're just using me to get to them huh?"

"Obviously. I mean you know this place better than just about anyone. Why should I have to do all the work when I have a local to do it for me?"

He chuckled. "You're a good person, you know that?"

"Yeah, I know. You're not so bad yourself."

Theo shook his head. "You know, I have to be honest. When you first told me what you do, I was skeptical. But I am starting to see why you're in the business you are. You're really good at this."

Gabrielle snorted. "If only I was as good at helping my own love life as I am at helping other people."

They stopped by the reception desk and the lights flickered and went out.

"Crap."

"What happened? Is it the storm?" Gabrielle asked.

"Probably not."

Patty clicked on a flashlight at the front desk. "You two okay?"

"Yeah. I'll go fix the fuse." Theo headed over to Patty and she handed him a second flashlight.

He walked back to Gabrielle. "It's fine. I'll go to take care of it."

"You know where the spare fuses are Theo?" His mom walked in carrying her own flashlight.

"Unless you moved them for the first time in twenty years."

"Need some help?" Gabrielle asked.

He squeezed her arm. "I got it. I know you've had a long couple of days. Patty can walk you back to your room."

Despite everything she'd told herself about not getting involved, she wasn't quite ready to leave Theo and go back to her room alone.

"Let me help. The sooner we finish the sooner I can get back and wash my hair."

THEO AND GABRIELLE RIFLED THROUGH THE crowded supply closet. Gabrielle scanned across boxes of toilet paper and cleaning supplies. Theo picked up a box, flashed his light in it and then set it back.

His brow wrinkled. "Mom has always kept them in here."

"Maybe they ran out," Gabrielle offered.

Theo snorted and pulled out another box. "Dad would never let that happen. He was an eagle scout at eleven. I started learning how to prepare for every disaster scenario imaginable when I was five."

Gabrielle closed a box and stood. "Well. I guess if we don't have power then we could just use candles and the fireplaces. It would definitely be more romantic."

"True." Theo looked at her in a way that no one had looked at her for a long time. Not that she'd given any guy a chance in the past two years. But for some reason, when Theo looked at her, it made her body tingle. She couldn't deny that she liked him looking at her that way.

Slowly he pushed her hair from her cheek. Gabrielle's body warmed at his touch and jackrabbits hopped circles in her stomach. She told herself not to enjoy it. Not to wonder what it would feel like to have his lips on her lips.

Theo moved slowly toward her, his gaze never left hers, as if asking permission with every inch they drew closer. Gabrielle took a step toward him and suddenly tripped over something. She lurched forward and Theo grabbed her before she hit the floor, slowing her fall. He tumbled on top of her and bumped the shelf behind them. Rolls of toilet paper rained down on his head. And a small box landed by his hand.

Gabrielle laughed, pinned under his weight. "Are you all right?"

He gave her a chagrinned smile. "I'm great. You?"

Gabrielle knocked into the box that had fallen next to them. The logo caught her eye.

"Oh! Are those them?"

"What?"

She grabbed the box of fuses and showed them to him.

Theo smiled. "I knew they were in here."

"Theo?" As if on cue his mom called to them from somewhere down the hall. "Gabrielle?"

Theo winked at her and then hopped to his feet. "Found em, Mom."

He offered Gabrielle his hand and pulled her to her feet as well. They stared at each other for a minute and Gabrielle couldn't decide if she was disappointed that he hadn't kissed her, or relieved. Getting close to Theo would definitely throw her off her game and distract her from what she'd been sent to do.

Gabrielle coughed and then he grabbed their flashlights and handed hers back to her.

Like it or not, she was definitely disappointed.

Theo read down the list of fuses in the power box while Gabrielle held a flashlight for him. He changed the appropriate fuse and then flipped the switch. Cheering and clapping could be heard from above.

"Guess all that zombie apocalypse training came in handy," she said.

Theo turned and they high-fived. "Don't tell my dad that or he'll have us all doing the training again."

THEO AND GABRIELLE WALKED INTO THE lobby where Ronald and Margery waited. Guests thanked them as they passed and Gabrielle made sure everyone knew it was all Theo.

"Not true," Theo retorted. "You're the one who found the fuses."

"Only because you bumped them down off the shelf."

"True but you stepped in the bucket," he pointed out.

"You both did it," said his mom.

113

"Partners in crime." Theo smiled.

"I knew those preparedness lessons would pay off sooner or later," said Ronald walking up to join them.

Gabrielle stifled a laugh.

"It was a fuse dad, not zombies."

"You know the Wentworths just couldn't stop raving about how much fun they are having this year," said Margery.

"Sometimes, because of day to day life, people lose touch with each other and grow apart. I like to think that I have a talent for helping them see the magic is still there. They just need to feed it a little."

"Kind of like this old lodge," said Margery.

"What do you mean?" Theo's brows furrowed.

"Your mom and I have been thinking about giving the lodge a makeover somehow," said Ronald. "Showing it the same TLC that Gabrielle is talking about."

"Like a remodel?" The concern in Theo's voice was palpable.

"Not a complete remodel. We can't afford that," said Ronald.

"But maybe just find some new things that we can offer our guests. Things to make their stay extra special. I think your dad and I have become like

Gabrielle said, losing touch because of the day-to-day things."

The look Theo threw her direction had her scrambling for something to say. "I didn't mean you," she blurted.

Margery squeezed her arm. "We know you didn't dear. It's just, the world has changed around us in the last twenty years. I think it's time we change with it."

"Like get a website and maybe some Wi-Fi in the rooms," said Ronald. "Possibly put in a pool."

Margery's eyes sparkled. "Who knows, maybe we will add a spa and some fun activities in the summer months."

"Like an adventure camp for kids," offered Gabrielle.

"That's a great idea," said Ronald.

"Whoa. Whoa. Whoa. Don't you think this is moving a little fast?" Theo asked.

Margery chuckled. "Sweetheart, we haven't even changed the wallpaper in fifteen years."

"Yes, but our guests come here because it's comfortable. It's what they know," Theo argued.

"But look what getting a little out of their comfort zone has done for the Wentworths." Margery kissed Theo's cheek. "I think we could all do with a little upgrade."

Gabrielle wondered what Margery meant, but she didn't get a chance to ask as Theo's parents walked away leaving a tense silence to fall between Theo and herself.

"I'm sorry," Gabrielle finally said. "I had no idea that this would have an impact on your parents."

He turned to her, his eyes full of conflict. "You know why I come here? Really come here every other week? It isn't because I have to do the books. I can do those for my parents online. I come because I want to get away from the city. Get away from the rush. Away from the fake people. The constant bombardment of ads telling me what I should be and who I should be."

"I get that-"

"Do you? My parents basically just said they want to turn this place into a what? A spa retreat for rich people? That's not what this place is. This is my home."

A pit grew in Gabrielle's stomach. "I don't think that's what your parents meant. I think they just want to try something new."

"And what if it doesn't work? What if they put all this time and money into changing this place and they don't get any new customers? The debt could crush them and they could end up losing their home."

"But what if it does work?" she offered. "What if it

brings new life into this place? What if it was amazing? Isn't that what you want? Don't you want them to succeed?"

Theo shook his head. "I... I have some accounting I need to finish up." He headed across the lobby to the stairs.

"Theo?" Gabrielle watched him go. "Theo I'm sorry!"

He headed up the stairs leaving her alone in the entryway, feeling suddenly very small.

Gabrielle shook her head and turned to go back to her room. All of the good feelings that she'd let bud inside her all came crashing down. Sigh... and once again her love curse struck again. Only this time it had struck before anything could even happen. Man, why couldn't she just keep her nose out of other people's business?

She needed to just do her job and get back home for Christmas. Once again, she reminded herself why she hadn't tried for a relationship with anyone in a long, long time. Because sadly, no good deed went unpunished.

Chapter Eleven

Gabrielle awoke to the buzzing of her phone. She groaned at the early hour and rolled over. The phone stopped and she sighed to herself and settled back into her pillow when it started buzzing again. Again, she grumbled but this time she looked at her phone. *Evie.*

Gabrielle grabbed the phone. "Hello?"

"There you are! I've been calling and calling."

Gabrielle swiped the sleep from her eyes. "What's up?"

"Is the date ready to go?"

Ready? No. She wasn't at all sure what to do for Chantel's special date. Everything they had done didn't seem like Chantel's speed at all. But Chantel had sent her to that specific lodge so clearly, she knew what the lodge had to offer, so maybe Gabrielle was on the right track after all.

Gabrielle got out of bed and walked to the window. Flurries of snow swirled in the air.

"Did the pass clear?"

"Not yet but Chantel wants an update."

Gabrielle stomped back to her bed and threw herself on it as her thoughts turned to Theo. "I'm getting ideas together."

"So, you know- you want them to do?"

Not again. Stupid connection. "I've been trying everything out myself, just like I always do and by the time you get here everything will be perfect."

"Chantel thinks- the pass- open- tomorrow morning. - tomorrow-noon. I'll call if- changes."

Gabrielle understood that both of their careers were on the line, but the frantic nature of her voice made Gabrielle begin to question if she'd done the right thing by taking Chantel's deal.

"See you tomorrow then," she said. "And bring me some clothes would ya? I seriously look like the ghost of Christmas past."

"What?"

"Bring me some clean-"

The line went dead just as Gabrielle's stomach growled. She stared at the phone for a minute and then crawled back under the covers. She wasn't ready to possibly run into Theo. Would he even want to help her anymore? She had no idea. Her stomach would have to wait.

An hour later Gabrielle walked through the lobby in another crazy Christmas outfit that resembled that of a Christmas tree. She looked around and her gut clenched. She felt terrible for the way they'd left things the night before. In the hour she'd spent laying in her bed that morning she'd decided to get back to the basics and focus on why she'd come to the lodge and nothing else. Not the Hart's Lodge problems, not any budding feelings for Theo, nothing. She had to focus and that's what she planned to do, right after she explained to Theo that she hadn't intended on his parents reacting the way they had.

But when she didn't see him in the lobby, she went and sat in a chair by the fireplace and dialed her mom's number. Surprisingly the call went through.

"Hi Mom."

"Hey Sweetie! How's the new client working out?"

"She hasn't shown up yet. I'm snowed in at the lodge while they're stuck in town."

"Are you going to make it out in time to help with the shelter?"

"I'm hoping no later than Monday or Tuesday. I promise I'll be there. We can wrap all day Wednesday and bake Thursday."

"Okay. But are you sure you're all right? You have power and food and everything?"

"Mom, I'm at a lodge, not the top of Mount Everest." She chuckled. "Tell dad to keep the checker board waiting."

"He already has it set up." Her mom paused for a moment. "Are you okay honey?"

Gabrielle's gut tightened. "Yeah. It's just…" She caught sight of Theo's broad shoulders and trim waist decked out in a thick flannel shirt, at the front desk. She stared at him for a moment as the knot tightened in her stomach like the wringing out of a wet towel. "Nothing. I'll see you in a few days, Mom. Love you."

Gabrielle hung up before her mom could ask her anything more. She did not want to get the barrage of questions that she'd be pelted with if she so much as mentioned a male's name. This… she would have to deal with on her own.

THEO FINISHED WITH PATTY AND TURNED TO see Gabrielle sitting by the fireplace. It looked like she'd found a spot to make her cellphone work.

She must have a great provider. Most cellphones couldn't even get half a bar up there.

She looked adorable in his sister's old Christmas tree sweater and green plaid leggings. She glanced over at him and he wanted to look away but he'd been spotted. *Busted.*

She threw him a small wave and Theo's gut twisted tight at the sight of her beautiful face. He'd been an ass the night before. It wasn't her fault his parents had wanted to update the lodge. Hell, he'd known they'd needed to do it for over a decade but change had never been his strong suit. Probably why he had taken so long to break things off with his ex. He'd known for months they weren't meant for each other but he'd been more afraid of starting over and finding someone else than trying to make it work. In the end, he just hadn't been able to deal with the growing differences between them.

"Hey." Theo shoved his hands in his pockets as he approached Gabrielle.

"Hey." She gave him a mild smile.

"About last night-"

"Theo, I'm really sorry. I didn't mean to-"

He held his hands up. "No, I'm sorry. I know you are only trying to help."

"I don't want to change this place. I promise. I love the charm of the lodge." Her eyes pleaded with him to believe her.

Theo's chest crushed inward. He sat next to her and stared into the fire for a moment trying to decide if he wanted to tell her the truth of why he'd gotten so upset. He looked into her soulfully earnest eyes and his gut fluttered like a first-time school boy crush.

"I know," he said. "It's just... I love the solitude of the lodge. The way it's kind of a world of its own. When I went off to college and got a job and got all caught up in all those things that detract from really living. I got so caught up in appearances that I forgot that life isn't meant to be perfect pictures. It's messy and complicated and an adventure."

"I get that."

He paused for a moment. "I used to date someone who complained when we went anywhere there wasn't Wi-Fi. I once tried to take her on the snowmobile and she was afraid because she might actually get snow on her new snowsuit."

Gabrielle's infectious smile crinkled the corners of her eyes. "I know people like that."

"Anyway. It was wrong of me to get angry with

you. My parents are right. We need to do something to update this place and try and get more business than just at Christmas. I just don't want to see it turn into one of those wheatgrass and kale juice only, toxin purging, salad bar, yoga farms."

Gabrielle snickered. "I'm pretty sure a website and some Wi-Fi won't turn it into one of those but I understand what you mean. When I was a kid, my dad used to take me to the drive-in movies every weekend. It was our favorite thing to do. Then one day they closed it down and put up a megaplex. It was a good theater. Comfortable seats. Air conditioning. Surprisingly, you could actually hear what the characters were saying. But it wasn't the same."

"So you forgive me for being a jerk?"

She looked at him for a moment. "Are we still going to lunch with the Wentworths?"

Without thinking Theo took her hand and squeezed it. "I wouldn't miss it."

She smiled and slid her hand out of his. "Then you are forgiven."

They stared at each other for a moment and his stomach dropped at the loss of her touch. He'd wanted to kiss her so much in the closet the day before.

For the first time he'd found a girl he could actually see himself wanting to build a life with. It was ridiculous since they'd only known each other a few days, but even so he couldn't deny that his feelings for Gabrielle were already stronger than anything he'd felt before. And surprisingly, that didn't scare him one bit. What scared him was the fact that she might not actually feel the same way. He just hoped that his stupidity from the night before had not ruined what chance he might have with her.

"Ready?" Jennifer asked, as she and Daniel walked into the room.

"Absolutely," Gabrielle replied, getting to her feet. "I'm starving."

"Every Christmas we go to McNaugty's Tavern to celebrate the anniversary of our engagement," said Jennifer.

"Wait. You got engaged up here?" asked Gabrielle.

"It's one of the reasons we still come every year."

"Let me get my coat," Gabrielle said.

"So, then Daniel is sitting at his desk waiting for his next appointment to show up and it's the guy from the parking lot."

"The one who stole your spot and laughed at you?" asked Gabrielle.

"Sure enough," said Daniel.

They all bursts out laughing.

"What did you do?" Theo asked.

"Nothing, said Daniel. "The moment the guy saw it was me he turned around and walked out."

Again they laughed.

Gabrielle swirled her straw in her soda. "I can't even imagine." Silence permeated the table for a moment and then Gabrielle raised her glass. "To the Wentworths. May every anniversary you have from here on out be as good as this one."

Jennifer squeezed Gabrielle's hand. "Thank you, sweetheart." Then she turned her gaze on Theo. "You might have just met, but take it from me, this one's a keeper." She winked at him.

Theo looked at Gabrielle. "I'm starting to think that too."

Gabrielle looked at him and then around the table. Her cheeks flushed a deep shade of petal pink. He wanted to take her hand in his again, but he remembered how she had pulled away from him that morning. He needed to do something to bring her back to where they had been before he'd gotten upset. He knew she'd been hurt by guys before, but he needed to show her he wasn't one of those guys. He was the right guy.

THE WENTWORTHS WALKED ARM IN ARM IN front of Theo and Gabrielle, down the sidewalk.

"The change in them is remarkable. If I hadn't seen it, I never would have believed it," said Theo.

"Sometimes all people need is a little nudge in the right direction."

"I feel like we've been nudged more than once in the last couple of days." Theo bumped her shoulder.

Gabrielle's cheeks warmed and she looked at her feet as they walked past a bakery. It had been less than a week. What kind of girl would he think she was if she told him that feelings were budding inside her like little tulips ready to burst open? For once she decided not to over think it. He'd said he liked her, why not tell him she felt the same?

Because you are cursed and though things are wonderful right now sooner or later they are bound to go bad and crush your heart again.

He smiled down at her and ran his fingers through his shaggy hair. "Do you mind? Being nudged in my direction?"

"Do you?" she asked, her stomach clenching.

"Oh! I haven't been ice skating since I was a little girl," said Jennifer stopping in front of a skating rink.

She turned to Theo and Gabrielle. "Will you go with us?"

"Us?" questioned Daniel.

Theo backed up a step. "Oh, I'm no good."

"Come on. I'll help you," said Gabrielle pulling him forward as Jennifer pulled on Daniel.

Theo gave a nervous laugh. "Are you any good?"

Gabrielle shook her head. "Nope."

JENNIFER HELPED DANIEL ACROSS THE ICE AS Gabrielle skated next to Theo who clung to the side of rink like it might run away from him leaving him stranded on a pool of ice.

"How is it possible that you grew up here and haven't ever gone ice skating?" Gabrielle asked.

"I never said I hadn't gone ice skating," said Theo. "I said I wasn't any good at it." He inched forward his skates barely moving on the ice.

"How do you know? You won't let go of the railing long enough to find out."

Theo looked up at her his eyes full of fear. "Because when I was nine my mom made me try out for the local hockey team. Let's just say if it wasn't for all the pads and the helmet, I'd have permanent brain damage."

"You mean you don't?"

He stopped and looked at her. "Haha."

Gabrielle laughed. "Let me help you."

"No thanks."

Seriously? He was going to pull out his male ego now?

"Daniel is letting Jennifer help him. If his ego can take being helped by a woman, I'm pretty sure yours can too."

Theo looked to the Wentworths and then back at her.

"Don't you trust me?" she asked.

Theo looked at her skeptically. Finally, he let go of the wall and took her hands.

Gabrielle skated backward as he pushed forward.

"How is it even possible you are good at this?" he asked.

Gabrielle shrugged and gripped his hands tighter as he lurched forward.

"Probably because I've tried so many things."

"Yeah? Like what?"

What had she not tried? "Rock climbing. Bungee jumping. Sky diving."

"Sky diving?"

"I'm not good at that apparently. As my now deaf jump instructor informed me."

Theo chuckled.

"I've been white water rafting, camping, and I ran a marathon. I wasn't good at that either."

"Didn't run fast enough?"

"Didn't finish. Turns out I don't like to run."

"Wow. You really have tried a lot of new things. Was it for work?"

"No. Personal."

Theo's eyebrows scrunched together. "I don't follow."

They'd fallen into a nice rhythm of him pushing forward as she pushed backward. Together they moved awkwardly around the rink.

"I have a tendency to date guys who I don't have much in common with. So, in an effort to make the relationship work I tried to like the things they liked."

"Did they ever try the stuff you liked?"

"Nope. Which is why we'd break up. I could never live up to the expectation of what they wanted me to be."

Theo stopped suddenly and opened his mouth but he pulled Gabrielle off balance. She tried to correct but like a character in a cartoon, his legs and skates had minds of their own as they flailed against the ice. She let out a cry as they both went down.

Gabrielle landed on his puffy down coat with a

grunt and then they laughed. "Wow, I feel like we've been here before recently."

"Almost like it's Déjà vu." She smiled and patted his chest. "I think I'm going to have to add ice skating to the 'not good at' pile."

Theo laughed and then his eyes grew serious. "For the record. I don't think there is anything you should change about yourself to please a guy."

Gabrielle licked her lips and despite the cool ice and air in the rink her body heated at his nearness. Again, thoughts of his lips on hers floated through her head.

Nope. Nope. Nope. She wasn't going to lose focus.

"Look. Look! I told you!" said Jennifer.

Theo chuckled and Gabrielle pushed off him as Daniel and Jennifer helped them back to their feet. Gabrielle and Theo looked at each other and then she looked away again.

Daniel kissed Jennifer on the cheek. "You're a pretty good matchmaker, you know that?"

Jennifer grinned from ear to ear. "Of course I am. I got you, didn't I?"

Chapter Twelve

G abrielle and Theo walked with Daniel and Jennifer toward the lodge.

Jennifer and Daniel continued up the steps. "Being around you two has been a breath of fresh mountain air," said Jennifer.

"You've helped us remember why we love each other," Daniel continued.

"We can never thank you enough for that," Jennifer finished.

"We didn't do anything more than fan the flames that you two spent over half your lifetimes building."

Jennifer walked to Gabrielle and hugged her before whispering something in her ear. Gabrielle smiled and nodded. Then Jennifer kissed them both on the cheek and together she and Daniel walked inside the lodge.

"What did she say to you?" Theo asked.

Gabrielle beamed up at him. "Nothing."

Theo wanted to press her but instead decided to let it go. She'd tell him when she was ready. "Okay. Keep your secrets."

Gabrielle took a step toward the lodge but Theo pulled her back. "Can I show you something before we go in?"

"Sure."

Theo pulled her to the side of the lodge, his heart pounding with each step closer he took to showing her his favorite spot. In all of his life, with all the girls he'd dated, he'd never before wanted to bring one of them to see his favorite spot, but for some reason he wanted to show Gabrielle. He wanted her to experience the joy and beauty that he felt every time he sat and stared down at the city below.

Theo led Gabrielle back behind the lodge. They passed the restaurant and out of the corner of his eye Theo caught a flurry of movement but he paid it no mind. He was so nervous he was afraid if he let anything distract him from the task at hand he might lose his nerve.

Out behind the lodge Theo took Gabrielle to a picnic bench, covered in snow, that overlooked the entire valley below. He brushed the snow off and they sat on the wooden table. Below them lay all the things he'd thought as a teen he wanted. But above them shone the things he prized most as an adult.

"It's breathtaking," said Gabrielle.

Theo wrapped his arm around her shoulders. She lay her head on his chest and they silently took in the view for a few minutes.

"This was always my favorite place as a kid," he finally said. "I used to sit here and look down at the city, imagining what people were doing down there. Eating out, going to movies, the mall, having fun. As a teen I couldn't wait to get out of here. I'd see all the other kids come up in their shiny cars and new skis and all I wanted was to go to college and become just like them. Money, parties, girls. I just knew I'd love it."

"I never would have guessed you were one of those guys."

Theo chuckled. "*Were* being the keyword."

She looked up at him. "What changed?"

Theo looked out over the city lights again. "After college I went to work for a big company and was living the material dream." He paused. How had he grown so close to her in such a short period of time? He'd not even told his ex his feelings before. But with Gabrielle, he wanted her to understand how he'd changed. Needed her to understand he wasn't that guy anymore. He wasn't like all the guys who had hurt her in the past. "About six months ago I started coming up here and I'd sit on this table and I realized I didn't look out at the city lights anymore. I looked up at the stars. I never really noticed them as a kid. From down there you can barely even see them. Over the last months I've found myself coming up here more and more to get away from the things that I used to think would make me happy."

Gabrielle lifted her head and stared at him. "But you're not one of those guys anymore? Not the one looking just for arm candy or not wanting to commit? Are you trying to tell me you're one of the good guys now?"

Theo chuckled. "Yeah, I guess I am. *Again.* I was a good guy all through high school and college but... Anyway. What I'm trying to say is... I like you Gabrielle. I know we haven't known each other that long but I feel a real connection to you."

"Something you've never felt before?" She cocked an eyebrow at him.

"I know it sounds cheesy but yes. I'll admit, my mom wasn't wrong when she said you aren't like the girls I've dated in the past. Sure, I admit I used to be a playboy who just wanted to have fun and not commit, but I'm not nineteen or twenty anymore. I'm a full-fledged adult and I want full-fledged adult things. Like a wife, and kids, and a dog and-"

"Whoa! Slow down."

"I'm just saying..." *What was he saying?* "I would never hurt you Gabrielle. And I don't want to lie to you about what I possibly see when I look at you. I won't rush you. I'm happy to wait. I just wanted you to know."

She blew out a breath and looked out over the city. She stayed silent for seconds that seemed to stretch out longer and longer, making Theo increasingly more nervous the longer she didn't say anything.

"I've dated so many guys who either don't want to commit, only care about their careers, or worse who do as little as they can to get by so they can spend their time partying."

"Well, I'm glad you didn't meet me a year ago. You'd never have given me a second glance. But like I said, I'm not that guy anymore."

"Then I'm glad I didn't too."

They stared at each other for a moment. The chemistry between them made Theo want to take her back to his room and lay her in his bed and in his arms, kissing her all night long.

Theo leaned closer to her. He brushed the hair from

her neck as he pulled her into a long slow kiss. The scent of the lodge's signature soap lingered on her skin and the feel of her plump lips on his had him pulling her closer.

His arms wrapped around her and he drew her even tighter.

"Thee Thee!" came a high-pitched voice.

Theo broke the kiss and jumped from the picnic table. "Oh no!"

"Theo?" Gabrielle asked, confusion played across her face.

He looked at Gabrielle's confused expression. He had less than ten seconds before they would be discovered, and there wasn't time to explain. But he needed to explain. He needed to explain before Chantel could ruin everything. Theo grabbed Gabrielle's hand and pulled her off the table.

"What's going on?" she asked.

"Thee Thee?" Chantel rounded the corner with Evie in tow. She squealed when she spotted Theo and ran to him. "Thee Thee!" She jumped and he let go of Gabrielle's hand just in time to catch Chantel mid leap.

Chantel planted a huge kiss on Theo.

Theo stiffened unable to process. Chantel smiled at him and rubbed her nose on his.

Theo blinked several times. "What... What are you doing here?"

"I'm here for you silly."

Theo set her on the ground and Chantel looked to Gabrielle. "I see you've met my... my friend Gabrielle."

Theo looked between them as Gabrielle's confused expression grew deeper.

"Your... friend?" he asked.

"Yes. I told her how amazing this place was and she said she just had to get away for a few days and come see it for herself." Chantel linked her arms in Theo's.

Theo swallowed hard as Gabrielle's eyes went to their linked arms and then her expression hardened.

"That's not exactly-"

"But Patty and your mom said there are no rooms available at all. So, I'm afraid I'm going to have to bunk in her room. You don't mind do you Gabrielle?"

Gabrielle looked from Evie to Chantel to Theo and then back to Chantel.

"Theo is your boyfriend?" Gabrielle said slowly.

Chantel put her head on his chest right where Gabrielle's had been minutes before. "My one and only true love."

Theo peeled away from Chantel. What was happening? He and Chantel hadn't been together in months and all of a sudden, she shows up at the Lodge calling him her true love? He needed to explain. He needed to understand himself. But most of all he needed Gabrielle to know that this wasn't what it looked like.

"What about the photo in your apartment? The one with the guy you were kissing on the cheek," Gabrielle asked, breaking the silence. "The blond guy with the sports car?"

Chantel scoffed. "That's my brother, Niles."

Theo took a step toward Gabrielle. "Gabrielle, I can explain."

Gabrielle backed up. "You want to explain why you are the boyfriend of my client?"

Theo stopped in his tracks. *Client? Chantel was her client? And now Chantel was at the lodge... that could only mean...* "Wait. So, all those things we did. Those perfect moments we had together were to create a date for her and me?"

Chantel whined and stepped forward. "You told him?"

Gabrielle's gaze moved to Chantel and she opened her mouth but Theo cut her off.

"Chantel. You hired this woman to create a date to propose?"

Chantel pouted and linked arms with him again. "Thee Thee, you and I belong together. You know it.

And I know it. I love you. But you've been dragging your feet so I thought maybe I'd nudge you so that I wouldn't have to wait any longer."

Theo extricated himself from her grip once more and shook his head. How had this happened? "Chantel, what part of me not returning your calls and not seeing you in over a month did you not understand?"

"You said you were busy."

"I was trying to be nice and give you space to move on. I thought you would get that."

Chantel's eyebrows slammed together and she looked at him like he'd suddenly sprouted flippers. "But... we're so picture perfect together."

"And that right there is the exact reason you and I don't belong together. I don't want posed and edited pictures of me plastered on Instachat. I don't want to be part of your polls and your fake tweets and your selfies and staged live streams and updates. I want..." He sighed. This wasn't the way he'd wanted this to go. He hadn't wanted to hurt Chantel- but it seemed being direct was the only way he was going to get her to see the truth. "I want a real life. Messy and fun and spontaneous. Not optimized for the best lighting."

Silence permeates the air.

"So... you don't want to marry me," Chantel finally said.

Theo could see the disappointment in her eyes. "I'm sorry Chantel. But I care for you enough to *not* ruin your life by marrying you when we don't belong together. It's why I told you three months ago that we needed to take a time out."

Chantel's mouth fell open and she closed it and opened it several times before finally shaking her head in disbelief.

Theo turned and looked at Gabrielle. She'd come to the lodge knowing Chantel had wanted to propose. She'd taken him out with the Wentworths and done everything he'd ever wanted a girl to do with him. Had it all been a lie? A setup so he would do those things with Chantel and fall for her pretending to want to do them? Had she been testing the waters to see if he would actually believe Chantel wanted those things? Theo's heart shattered like it'd been smashed with a baseball bat.

He swallowed hard and then shook his head. "I'll tell you one thing, Gabrielle, you're more amazing at your job than I originally thought because, you did it. You created the perfect harmony of activities to make a guy fall hard. Only, it wasn't for you was it? The whole time you were just setting things up for Chantel. What were you hoping to find all my favorite things so you could run and tell her so she could manipulate me into thinking she loved them too?"

"Wait. You think I knew you were dating her? Do you really think I would have told you all that stuff about myself if I knew you were dating someone else? Is that the kind of girl you think I am? After everything I told you about my ex? I told you I didn't want the kind of guy who could do that stuff."

Theo stared at her not knowing what to believe. How could she not have known he was the one Chantel wanted to propose to? Everyone had known he'd dated her for the last year. Complete strangers had followed him on the street peppering him with questions on a regular basis. It was impossible for her to not have known, right?

"Wow. Just... wow." Gabrielle shook her head and crossed her arms over her chest. Her gaze hardened on him. "I guess you weren't the only one that was wrong. All that bull about being a good guy and having changed. That's all it really was, wasn't it? Just a load of bull."

Unable to form words Theo turned and stomped off toward the lodge. He had no idea what to believe. Was it possible Gabrielle hadn't known about him and Chantel? Had Chantel really thought they were still together and that sending a girl up to find out what he loved to do would make him want to marry her?

Theo opened the door to the lodge and stepped inside.

"Theo! There you are," said his mom. "I need to warn you. Miss Aromatherapy is back."

Theo continued past her without even looking up. "Thanks mom, but she already found me."

GABRIELLE STARED AFTER THEO. HOW COULD he possibly think she would do something so deceitful? Maybe because he himself had been deceitful with her. He'd kissed her and told her he had feelings for her while being together with Chantel. He'd listened to her talk about her ex and what he'd done to her and the whole time he'd had a girlfriend back in the city. A very influential girlfriend. A girlfriend who-

Chantel stepped closer to Gabrielle and her heart plummeted to her stomach. "When I tell my followers that you stole my man, you'll never work again."

"Chantel, I didn't know that was your guy," said Gabrielle trying to at least keep Chantel from destroying her.

"Save it," said Chantel. "You think I'm going to

believe anything you tell me? Theo said that you did everything to make him fall for you. Was that a lie?"

"No. I mean yes. I mean…" Gabrielle took a deep breath.

Chantel held up her hand. "Save it. I don't care either way," said Chantel. "You promised me a perfect date and you didn't give me one. In my book, that is a failure."

Evie stepped up for the first time. "Chantel, please, wait a minute."

Chantel spun around and looked at Evie. "I'm sorry, do I know you?" she asked in a sickly-sweet tone.

Chantel stomped off before Evie could respond.

Gabrielle watched her go and with her, all the hopes and dreams she had for the future and her business.

Evie rushed to her side. "I am so sorry Gaby. I truly am. I-"

Gabrielle couldn't take any more. Theo was gone. Her business was gone. She had nothing now. Absolutely nothing.

Without a word she turned and walked the other direction.

Chapter Thirteen

The next morning Gabrielle stood outside the lodge waiting for her ride to come. She'd barely slept the night before. Instead, she'd spent most of it tossing and turning and trying to figure out how she had been so stupid as to not have realized Theo had been Chantel's intended fiancé.

He'd talked about his ex, but she'd always assumed the ex was just that, an ex. And how stupid was Theo that he thought that just because he hadn't talked to Chantel in a month that she would think they were broken up? Chantel wasn't the kind of girl to take hints easily. But even with all of that, what got at her the most was the fact that he actually thought Gabrielle was the kind of person who would know-ingly try and get to know him for money.

At seven that morning she'd ordered a car to come pick her up. She'd changed out of Theo's sister's clothing. Neatly folded them and placed them in a pile on the perfectly made bed and had gathered her purse and belongings and slipped out the front of the lodge without seeing anyone.

She stood in the frosty morning air, stamping her feet and watching the progress of her ride on the app on her phone when she heard a set of luggage wheels roll out the front door. Undeterred, Gabrielle refused to turn and see who it was.

The sounds of the bag banging down the sets told Gabrielle exactly who it was. There was only one person she knew who could beat up luggage that forcefully without even meaning to.

Evie stopped next to Gabrielle; shoulders hunched like a whipped puppy. The two share a tense silence as Gabrielle looked at her app again.

"I brought your suitcase," Evie offered lamely.

Great. So, it was *her* suitcase taking the beating.

The car was only five minutes out. Five minutes. She just had to make it through five minutes.

"I'm really sorry," Evie blurted on the verge of tears. "I didn't know this would happen, Gabs."

Gabrielle turned off her phone and sighed. "You didn't know that I would spend several days up here with her sort-of boyfriend and totally fall for him, only to have him think me a fake, and storm off while your boss single-handedly destroys what little reputation I have?"

Evie looked at her with tear rimmed eyes. "Yeah. That."

Gabrielle shook her head and snorted. She reached out and pulled Evie into a hug.

"It's not your fault."

Evie grabbed onto her tight. "I've ruined your business."

A smirk crossed Gabrielle's face. "Okay, it's a little your fault."

A small fuel-efficient car pulled up in front of the lodge and a man hopped out.

"Gabrielle?"

She nodded and pointed to the bag she'd been hoping to have arrive for days. The driver grabbed Gabrielle's bag and put it in the car. Gabrielle followed him and stopped before getting in the backseat.

"You want a ride?"

Evie's face lit up. "Yes please. Chantel took all the bags. Including the one that had my wallet and phone in it."

Gabrielle shook her head and got into the vehicle. She scooted over and Evie slid in and hugged her tight.

"I really am sorry about Theo too. For what it's worth I think you guys would have been perfect for each other. Way better suited than Chantel and Theo... well, the Theo he is now anyway. Chantel thought it was just a phase but he's really changed a lot in the last six months."

Gabrielle swallowed hard and looked out the window. That's what she had thought too.

THEO SAT IN FRONT OF THE FIREPLACE staring at the photo of him, Gabrielle, Daniel and Jennifer on his phone. He wore the same clothes from the night before. Having gotten no sleep, he'd spent the night down at a local twenty-four-hour coffee shop in town, doing the one thing he hated most- surfing social media. He'd looked up Gabrielle everywhere he could find her. He'd scrolled through hundreds of photos of people she'd helped set up dates for. He perused every one of her reviews. He watched happy couples get married and thank her for her help. He even found a photo of her with her ex. He hated to admit that it pained him a bit to see them smiling together and happy. Everything that there was online to learn about her, he'd learned. And the pang of guilt that struck him for having jumped to conclusions about her made him realize just how far he still had to go to becoming a better person.

"Theo!" Jennifer and Daniel walked in dressed for the ski slopes.

Theo looked over. "Hello Mr. and Mrs. Wentworth."

Jennifer gave him a stern look. "I thought we were past that."

Theo nodded. "Sorry."

Jennifer and Daniel exchanged a look. "I didn't know if you and Gabrielle had plans today but we thought we might try skiing if you want to come with us."

Theo looked at his phone even though he'd already shut it off. "Thank you but I don't think so."

"You can't possibly be as bad at it as you are at ice skating. Come on," said Daniel. "If two old geezers like us can try it after all this time you shouldn't be scared."

Jennifer smacked him playfully. "Who are you calling an old geezer?"

"Uh... Did I say old geezer? I mean us young, spry, beautiful, intelligent-"

Jennifer chuckled. "Yeah, yeah, that's good."

They kissed and Theo's gut twisted remembering the feel of Gabrielle's lips on his.

"Thank you. Really. But I can't," he said.

"That's too bad. Well, have you seen Gabrielle?" asked Jennifer.

"I was told she checked out a few hours ago."

"She's gone?"

"Yeah. She went to her parents for Christmas."

Daniel and Jennifer exchanged a look and then Jennifer sat next to Theo. "What did you do?"

"Believe it or not, I'm the victim in this case. Gabrielle came up here to arrange a date for my ex-girlfriend so she could propose to me."

"Wait. Gabrielle knew you were dating someone and she had you go out with us all those days anyway?"

Theo ran his fingers through his hair and then rubbed his face remembering the sincerity in Gabrielle's soulful eyes. "I... I don't know. I don't think so, but how can I believe her when her whole job is a ploy to get people to think they're in love and get engaged?"

"Is that what you think she did for us?" asked Daniel. "She made us think we were in love?"

"You guys are different. You were already in love."

"What's to say the people she helps aren't already in love too?" asked Jennifer. "Did she do anything while you were together to make you think that she was deceitful or dishonest? Seems to me a girl like

Gabrielle wouldn't try and break up a relationship if she knew the guy was already with someone else. And I doubt very highly she would put her heart out there to be broken once again."

Theo looked at Jennifer for a long beat. "You think she put her heart out there?"

Jennifer patted Theo's shoulder. "Sweetheart everyone who saw you two together couldn't help but see you are perfect for each other. That doesn't just happen when people are being deceitful."

"Grandma!" Preston ran in the room and launched himself into her arms.

"Hello, Lovie."

Willis walked up and shook hands with Daniel.

"Mom? Dad? Is everything okay? We weren't planning on coming until Tuesday."

"Everything's just fine," said Daniel.

"We thought maybe today we'd come up and going skiing with you," Jennifer said to Preston.

Preston's eye widened like bright blue tree ornaments. "Really?"

"Really," said Daniel.

"Then tomorrow maybe we can go snow-mobiling. Or ice skating," Jennifer offered.

Preston's eyes narrowed on his grandmother. "You aren't dying are you?"

Jennifer laughed. "What? Why would you ask that?"

"I just want to make sure you aren't doing a bucket list thing because you're going to die."

Jennifer pulled Preston in for another hug and kissed him hard on the cheek. "No sweet boy. We aren't dying. At least not anymore."

She reached out and Daniel kissed her hand.

Willis looked between them and smiled. "Maybe I should come to this lodge next year."

Daniel grabbed Preston and set him on his feet. "Race you to the car."

Preston took off with Willis and Jennifer's face lit up as she watched them go. She turned back to Theo and gave him a sympathetic smile and took his hands in hers.

"Go get her. If you don't, you'll regret it for the rest of your life." She kissed his cheek and then stood. "Oh, and bring a gift. A good one."

Daniel took her hand. "When you're done with that. I want to run something by you and your folks. I think I might be able to help get some more people up here."

"Thanks, Daniel."

Daniel and Jennifer walked out arm in arm.

Theo watched them and then turned back to the

fireplace. He spotted the large Christmas tree in the corner and looked up at it, remembering the moments he spent with Gabrielle picking it out, cutting it down and decorating it with his parents.

Patty approached him dragging a suitcase behind her and carrying a purse. "Hey do you know a Evie Lopez?"

"Yeah, she's Chantel's assistant."

"Her bag and her purse were in the lost and found. What should I do with them?"

Chapter Fourteen

Gabrielle sat curled up in her dad's large overstuffed chair thumbing through Chantel's Instachat. There were hundreds of photos of her and Theo. Older photos where Theo was partying and dancing and happy, but newer photos where he was posed but not as happy while Chantel remained oblivious. And finally, photos from the last months of Chantel alone or reposts of her and Theo from the year before.

Each one picture perfect. Expertly lit. Makeup flawless. Settings decorated meticulously like they'd been designed by Grant Conlee. All the things Gabrielle wasn't. Hell, if she got a selfie where she was actually looking at the camera and not looking confused because she couldn't hit the photo button, smile and look at the right spot all at the same time- she called that a win.

Her dad walked in the room. "Hey baby girl."

Gabrielle looked up at him and gave him a mild smile. "Hey dad."

He kissed her head and then sat on the couch.

"Your mom and Evie are in there making dinner. I have all the presents sorted by gender and age ready to be wrapped."

She sipped her cider. "Great. Thanks."

"I'm really sorry things didn't work out for your business. That girl had no right to say those things about you."

Gabrielle shrugged, the memories of Chantel's blazing rant on Yelp as well as her social media page from the night before burned into her mind.

"It doesn't matter." She stared out the front window into the neighbor's blinking Christmas lights. Across the street, a giant blow up Santa waved at her.

"What are you going to do?" her dad asked.

"Go back to school. Find a job. I'm not sure."

Her dad sat for a moment. "I'd offer for you to stay with us for a while but I'm not going to."

Gabrielle looked over to see if he was joking. His expression said he wasn't. "You aren't?"

"Nope. Because the Gabrielle I raised isn't a quitter. She isn't someone who would let a woman who makes her money by getting fist bumps from strangers on the internet bully her into quitting not only what she loves, but what she is amazing at."

Gabrielle smiled. He'd always been great with the tough love. "Thanks dad. But who is going to want to hire a special date consultant that they think might steal their boyfriend?"

"Is your usual clientele the kind who follows or listens to someone named Chantel Blue?"

Gabrielle laughed. "Probably not."

"Then what's the problem? You had a bad client. You can't please everyone, Gabs. I'm proud of you. You're doing what you've always been meant to do. Making a difference in people's lives." He stood to go and then turned back to her. "I bet if you look at that page you have up there on that social thing you'd be surprised."

"What do you mean?"

Her dad picked up her laptop and handed it to her. "Take a look for yourself."

Gabrielle put down her cider and opened her computer. On her business page Chantel's 1 star rating stared at her as boldly as if Chantel had taken a photo of her perfectly manicured nails flipping Gabrielle off. Gabrielle swallowed hard and scrolled down. To her surprise there were dozens of comments from people she'd helped. Photos of them married. Happy. With their babies. All telling Chantel off.

Tears flooded Gabrielle's eyes. She had three new messages. She clicked on them one by one. They were all guys asking for her help setting up a special date.

Gabrielle laughed and swiped the tears from her eyes. Her dad was right. What did it matter what Chantel said? After all, she didn't usually have female clients anyway. And she'd worked damn hard to build her business. Why was she ready to throw in the towel at the very first sign of dissatisfaction – especially when it wasn't even her fault?

No. She would not let Chantel win. She might have to get a business loan. Pay for ads. Get a real mailing address and more but she was prepared to do it. She refused to let Chantel Blue ruin the one thing that had made her happier than anything else in her life.

After Gabrielle finished replying to her messages and set up meetings for all three new clients, the doorbell rang.

"Gabs can you get that?" Evie called.

"Seriously?" she asked. Gabrielle shook her head

and walked to the front door. Smiling she pulled open the door. Her smile wavered as she stared at the tall handsome man peering at her shyly.

"Hi," Theo finally said.

Gabrielle's heart thundered so hard she wondered if it was trying to kill her.

"How... How did you find me?"

Theo pulled up Evie's suitcase. "Evie's bag and purse were in the lost and found and I went through her phone and found your parents' home number so I called and talked to your mom."

Gabrielle looked over her shoulder in time to see her mom and Evie duck out of sight. *Of course they would be behind this setup.*

"You didn't have to come all this way to drop those off. Evie could have driven up to get them."

"But then I wouldn't have gotten to see you."

Memories of his hurtful words the night before floated to the forefront of her mind. "I thought you didn't want anything to do with me. Seeing as how I'm a liar and manipulator and everything."

"I didn't mean that," he pleaded. "I was just so... shocked."

"What do you think I was? I told you about my past. I told you I don't do the two girls thing and then all of a sudden a girl pops up, jumps into your arms and kisses you. Just seconds after I let you kiss me, I might add."

A thick tension fell between them.

"I know and I'm sorry. I really did consider Chantel and I broke up. I get that I should have been clearer with her about it, but in my eyes we were through. She was everything I had decided I didn't want."

"You say that but she sure thought you two were still together. How can I know for certain that you weren't just testing the waters to see if there was something better out there or not?"

Even as Gabrielle said the words, she didn't want to believe them. She couldn't believe them. Couldn't believe that he was that kind of person. Couldn't believe that she'd fallen for another total loser. Couldn't believe that she was really and truly cursed in the love department.

Theo blew out a heavy breath. "I guess you'll have to trust me."

"Like the way you trusted me when I said I had no idea you were the one I was sent up there to get engaged?"

Gabrielle's heart told her that he hadn't done what her ex had. That he hadn't tried to play both sides of the fence. That he was one of the good ones. But her head told her to be smart. If he could jump to conclusions about her so easily once, he could do it again.

"Gabrielle, I told you I was not the same person I used to be and for the most part I'm not. But I still have my faults. I still jump to conclusions about people's motives. I'm better, but I'm not perfect. I can't promise you it will never happen again; all I can promise is that I am trying."

Gabrielle bit the inside of her cheek. Her heart battled with her head. She wanted to take the leap. Put herself out there. Give him a chance, but with everything she'd been through... and now she was going to have to work even harder at her business. She didn't even know if she had time for a relationship.

"Uh... so, I... I wanted to bring these by for Evie, and give you this." Theo pulled a small box from behind his back and handed it to her.

"You didn't have to do that." Her heart screamed at her to forgive him.

"Well... I'll let you go. I know you and your dad have a lot to do before Christmas Eve."

Gabrielle stepped out and took the suitcase and purse from him. Theo gave her a small wave and headed down the walkway as Gabrielle looked at the package.

"What's wrong with you?" her mom whispered.

Gabrielle turned to her mom and Evie in the kitchen doorway again.

"He just drove three hours in the snow. Do you really think he came just to drop those off?" Evie said. "I mean he's a great guy and all but seriously?"

Gabrielle looked at Theo's broad shoulders as he approached his car. Conflict swirled inside her as she realized she not only wanted to believe him, she did believe him. She set everything down and ran out the door.

"Wait!"

Theo stopped.

Gabrielle raced down the sidewalk toward the car and slipped as she got to him. He caught her and their eyes locked.

"I was an idiot," he admitted.

Gabrielle nodded. "You were."

"I didn't listen."

"No, you didn't."

"I said horrible things."

"You did."

"Are you going to keep agreeing with me?"

She smiled. "As long as you keep telling the truth."

Theo helped her get settled back on her feet. "Well, then the truth is... I think I'm in love with you."

Gabrielle's heart squeezed so tight she was sure she'd pass out. "You do?"

"I love how your arms feel around me when we snowmobile. And I love the way your eyebrows crease together when you are coming up with an idea. And I love how you try to lead me around the ice-skating rink. And I love, love, love the way you try to help others find true love without once thinking about yourself."

"Yeah, I love those things about me too."

Theo pulled her closer.

"And if we're being totally honest, you're not so bad yourself." Gabrielle leaned into him.

"That's all I get? I say all those nice things about you and-"

She yanked him in and smashed her mouth into his. A whoop and holler came from the door and they turned to see Evie, her mom and dad in the doorway, clapping.

Theo hugged Gabrielle and they both laugh. Being in his arms felt righter than anything she'd felt in her entire life. And in that moment, she knew she loved him too.

"Well, are you going to bring the boy in the house so we can meet him?" her dad called.

THEO COULDN'T BELIEVE THE FEELING OF relief and joy that settled in his bones at the touch of Gabrielle's fingers entwined with his again. He needed to talk to her. To explain how being around too many fake people for too long had colored his views. Had jaded him and caused him to jump to conclusions. But that in the future he would do his damndest to see people for the good they did. She needed to know those things- but not at that moment. At that moment he needed to put on his big boy pants and get ready to meet her parents. He'd already spoken to her mom on the phone and her mom had been as understanding and kind as Gabrielle, but he had the feeling her father might be a tougher cookie.

"Dad, this is Theo," said Gabrielle as they walked through the door.

"Pleased to meet you, sir." Theo stuck out his hand.

Her dad eyed him for a moment. "So, you're the one who made my daughter come home in tears."

"Dad-"

"No. It's okay. I deserve that." Theo straightened and looked her father in the eye. "Yes, sir. I was the idiot who did that."

Her dad looked Theo up and down. "You're not going to do that again, right?"

"No, sir. Not if I can help it."

"And there are no other girlfriends out there who don't realize you broke up with them previously, right?"

"Yes, sir. I mean no, sir?" Theo looked to Gabrielle and then back at her dad. "I mean, yes, there are no other girls."

"Can you wrap presents?"

"Uh... yes?"

"Well, all right then." Her dad clapped him on the shoulder. "You may come in, but only because we can use all the hands we can get to help wrap these presents."

Theo smiled and shook her dad's hand. "Fair enough."

THE EVENING PASSED QUICKLY WITH ALL OF them wrapping presents, making cookies and getting everything ready to take to the kids for Christmas Eve. The longer Theo sat with Gabrielle and her family the more it felt to Theo like he'd always been meant to be there. Her father regaled them with stories of when Gabrielle was little and Gabrielle in turn talked about the time her dad had almost blown himself up with the gas grill. Every moment together made Theo smile bigger than the last. It was just like being home with his own family for the holidays.

After a while Gabrielle's mom, dad and Evie headed up to bed and Gabrielle and Theo snuggled on the couch with a bowl of popcorn and a Christmas romance movie.

"You know these things all end up the same, don't you?" he asked.

"What do you mean?"

"They end up coming together. Getting over their differences and falling in love."

"So? Just because you know it's going to end happily doesn't mean you don't enjoy the journey along the way."

"True." He tilted her chin and kissed her. The salty taste of popcorn lingered on her lips. "Are you going to open my present?"

"But I didn't get you anything. I feel bad."

"Everything I want for Christmas is right here."

He kissed her again and then reached over and picked up the small box he'd brought and handed it to her.

Gabrielle looked at the box and then unwrapped it.

Her eyes widened and a smile spread across her lips. "Theo." She laughed as

she pulled the small sweater ornament from the box. "Where in the world did you find another one of these?"

"My mom made an extra one for each of us. To give to someone special when the time came."

No, he wasn't asking her to marry him, not yet, but he wanted to make sure that his intentions were crystal clear.

Gabrielle's cheek deepened and then she kissed him. "Will you put it on the tree for me?"

Theo took the sweater and walked to the tree.

"No. Not there," said Gabrielle.

He moved it.

"More to the right."

Amused, he moved it.

"Wait. To the left."

He moved it again.

"Wait."

"Gabrielle!"

"There. There is perfect."

She joined him at the tree. He wrapped his arm around her waist and they stared at the tree.

"So how long are you staying? I don't want you to miss Christmas with your family."

"I figured I'd stay long enough to see you dressed up like an elf and to convince you to say yes to the idea I had on my drive down."

Gabrielle looked at him skeptically. "Idea? What kind of idea?"

Theo grinned. "A job offer."

Epilogue

ONE YEAR LATER

Theo walked across the snow with a group of kids. "Okay everyone. This way to snowman building class." He looked around the group. "Preston?"

Preston popped out of the group and ran forward, beaming.

"Preston is our Jr. Lodge Chaperone. You're going to follow him to meet Miss Patty for snowman building fun. Okay?"

The kids nodded.

Preston straightened and pushed his shoulders back. "All right everyone follow me. Single file. That's right. Come on."

Theo looked at Preston and gave him a thumbs up. He looked at his watch and baby foxes somersaulted in his stomach. *Almost time.*

THEO STEPPED INTO THE LODGE AND STOPPED in the doorway of the craft room where his mom sat at an easel with several couples giving an art class. He smiled and continued onward to the ballroom where music floated out. Daniel and Jennifer walked around a classroom of couples, including their son Willis and a pretty woman, straightening arms, moving shoulders and positioning everyone just right before resuming their own position and beginning their dance instruction.

Things really had changed in the last year. They'd upgraded the lodge in small ways while keeping all the appeal and charm that it had always had. They offered Wi-Fi in the bedrooms, but also shut off the Wi-Fi for certain amounts of time during the day and evening to ensure people spent more time outside their rooms than inside.

They offered a myriad of new classes and excursions for both adults as well as kids. But his favorite addition to the lodge, and the most popular, sat right across the room from him, talking to a client.

He leaned against the wall and watched Gabrielle look through a large binder with one of the lodge guests.

"I think that would be an excellent choice, Charlie. We could do breakfast in the gazebo, and then the snow-mobiling with the picnic up to Lovers Peak, and there we will have a blanket and champagne already waiting for you. My assistant Evie will be just out of sight waiting for your signal to bring in the dessert and the ring."

"Sounds perfect," Charlie smiled.

"We'll set everything up and see you on Thursday."

Charlie shook her hand. "Thank you so much. I know how booked you are but I'm really grateful you could squeeze me in."

Gabrielle nodded. "Our pleasure."

Charlie walked off as Theo crossed to Gabrielle and hugged her. "How's it going?"

"Busy. The entire schedule is booked through New Year and we are already getting reservations for Valentines. I have a bunch of new ideas. Like a Queen of Hearts ball and maybe a horse drawn carriage ride through town, and-"

"And here I was hoping you'd be free for a few minutes. Or maybe an hour."

She looked at her watch. "I do need to take lunch but the Miller party's special food order should be being delivered in about forty-five minutes. Why? What's up?"

"A surprise."

Gabrielle looked up at him skeptically as Evie arrived.

"Do you know anything about this?"

"About what?" Evie asked.

"About a surprise?"

"Surprise? Who me? Nope." Evie put on her most innocent expression.

"Evie?"

Evie took a step backward. "Is that Margery calling? I think that's Margery calling me." She ran out.

Gabrielle turned back to him. "What are you up to?"

Theo reached into his pocket and pulled out a blindfold.

THEO LED GABRIELLE BLINDFOLDED OUTSIDE and she fought the anxiety building inside her at not knowing what was going on.

"Are we done?" she asked.

"Not yet," said Theo.

A moment passed and then another. Someone rushed by and then Theo leaned in close, his breath tickling her neck.

"All right." Theo took off Gabrielle's blindfold.

She blinked against the bright sun as she registered his favorite table overlooking the city setup with china and champagne flutes and an elegant lunch.

Gabrielle laughed as her stomach growled. "What's this?"

Theo wrapped his arms around her waist from behind and kissed her ear. "It's for you."

"What's the occasion?" she asked as he led her to the table and pulled out a chair for her.

Theo's jaw dropped in mock offense. "Don't you remember?"

Gabrielle wracked her brain. What had she missed?

"Exactly one year ago today we met."

"That's today?" She felt terrible. "I've been so busy I totally forgot." For someone who was great at making special days for other people she sure was lousy at doing it for herself.

"I didn't." Theo got down on one knee and pulled out a box.

Gabrielle gasped. They'd talked and talked about getting engaged but they'd said they wanted to wait until her business was doing better. And yes it had grown exponentially in the last year but... she still hadn't expected this.

"Gabrielle, a year ago you gave me the best Christmas I've ever had. I want to give you the same for the rest of our lives."

Gabrielle teared up.

"Gabrielle Miller, will you marry me?"

"Yes. Yes. A thousand times, yes!"

He slipped the ring on her hand and suddenly everyone was there, cheering and clapping for them. Her parents. His parents. The Wentworths. Evie. Even Theo's sister in one of her crazy Christmas sweaters.

Theo kissed her. "I love you."

GABRIELLE JUMPED UP AND HUGGED HIM. They fell to the ground and Evie snapped a photo as Gabrielle showed the ring on her hand.

"Now that's a photo worthy of social media," said Evie.

"Yes, send it to me so I can post it on the website," said Margery.

"And to me," said Jennifer.

"And me as well," said Theo.

"I thought you didn't have any social media accounts," said Gabrielle.

"But now I have a reason to. To show off my beautiful future wife."

The End

Rekindling Christmas

By Rebekah R. Ganiere

Chapter One

J esse strolled down the chilly street, his boots crunching on the packed snow that blanketed every surface in a fabric of shimmering white and filled him with nostalgia. He hadn't seen snow in over a decade.

He passed the old familiar bookstore, flooded with memories of the last time he'd been inside hiding amongst the stacks of books, lips locked on the beautiful brunette that should have been his wife. His gut clenched and the corners of his mouth tugged down. Jesse shook his head, driving the memory down where he kept all his regrets, and continued down the sidewalk.

A group of young college girls slowed as he passed

them. Their mouths fell open slightly and Jesse struggled to keep from blushing.

"Afternoon ladies." He nodded, and the group raced off giggling.

Jesse shook his head. Guess he wouldn't be able to avoid his past and be as invisible in town as he'd hoped.

The thought of fresh doughnuts and cocoa pulled him closer to 'Showtunes Bakery'- the small mom and daughter bakery where every doughnut and drink was named after a classic Broadway show.

He headed for it and his knee buckled in front of the Johnson's pharmacy. Jesse gripped the edge of the wooden bench before he stumbled to the ground.

Dammit.

The doctor had told him it was too soon to go without his brace.

Jesse brushed the snow from the bright red bench and sat down heavily. His knee ached from his trek around town. He spotted the city hall clock. He'd only been out thirty minutes. At this rate he was never going to heal. He sighed and rubbed his leg through his jeans trying to ease the sore muscles.

All around him people strolled up and down the street. Into shops, out of shops. Cups of coffee steaming in their hands. Some laden down with bags and packages for the upcoming holidays. Christmas music played in the park from the ice rink that the city erected every winter. With Thanksgiving only three days past, the city wasted no time in getting ready for the holidays.

He shut his eyes and took a deep breath. It'd been almost fifteen years and still nothing had changed. The smells, the sounds, the atmosphere. All of it. Home.

"Hello."

Jesse opened his eyes to see a little girl with long blonde hair and bright blue eyes sitting next to him.

He smiled. "Hey."

She held a plant shaped like a Christmas tree in her bare hands. "Merry Christmas."

"Merry Christmas to you too."

Her bright purple leggings clung to her legs and tucked into snow boots. A long purple striped sweater coat hardly seemed warm enough to keep out the chill. Jesse scanned the street.

"Are your mom and dad here? I think you need a coat."

She smiled. "The cold doesn't bother me. I've always lived here."

"I've been away for a while. Guess I'm not used to it anymore."

She nodded. "Being down south in the sun has made you more sensitive probably."

Jesse snorted. She sounded much more mature than possible for such a young girl.

"I know who you are," she said. "Everyone does. You're the famous football player my mom talks about. She watches all your games. You're impressive."

His gut tightened at the thought that he'd never play again. "I *was* impressive."

She watched Jesse rub his knee. "Did you get hurt?"

"Yup. I'm done with football. Well, playing anyway."

The little girl stood. "My mom will be sorry to hear that."

She held out her small plant. Its piney fragrance drifted back to him hitting him with a sense of longing.

"This is for you."

"I can't take it. It's yours."

"Actually, It's not." she said.

Jesse took the plant. "I'm sorry-"

He looked up again, but the little girl was gone.

Jesse stood and spun in a circle. He caught a glimpse of a purple striped sweater skipping down the street. He opened his mouth to call to her, but the girl disappeared around the corner.

Jesse shook his head. *Weird.*

The smell of doughnuts made his stomach growl. He turned and limped toward Showtunes.

"ANNIKA?" THE SOUND OF HER NAME MADE Annika stop reading, though her eyes didn't lift from the page of her book.

His voice still held the same husky, deep tone that rumbled in the air and got the attention of every woman in the vicinity. The one that made her weak in places that weren't lady-like and flush in places that weren't convenient.

Her heart thundered as she tried to figure out what to do. He'd said her name thousands of times– but not in a long, long time.

"Anna."

She lifted her eyes, and in front of her stood an All-American-good-looking-farm boy with the heart-stealing-smile– the same smile that had stolen her heart her first year of college and broken it two years later when he'd gone off to play for the NFL.

Annika collected her thoughts and gave him a polite, yet not overly eager smile. "Jesse Winchester."

She had to keep her composure. She couldn't dare lose it in front of everyone in town. She'd be the center of the monthly professor gossip circle at school and she'd had enough of those clucking hens for one lifetime.

"Annika Jolley. I can't believe I'm seeing you." His dimpled cheeks were darn near as perfectly kissable as she'd remembered.

Memories and feelings she'd buried for a decade and a half bubbled to the surface. She glanced around the doughnut shop for someone, anyone, she could pretend to be meeting- but there was no escape.

"What are you doing in town?" she asked. "I thought you were off playing football somewhere in Dallas, or something." She let the lie roll off her tongue like wine. She knew very well that Jesse hadn't been playing in Dallas since the previous season.

"Blew out my knee and got myself traded. Now that it looks like I might be out for good, I decided to come back."

"Sorry to hear that." She gripped her cup of pumpkin spiced cocoa so tight it crushed inward. "Is the school doing a fundraiser this weekend or something?"

He shifted a potted rosemary plant from one hand to the other. "No fundraiser. I wanted to finish my degree."

"Really?" She sipped again trying to keep from

racing out the door or smashing him in the face with the cup. "I'm surprised they didn't ask you to coach."

"Oh, they did. I start coaching in the spring and I'll pick up a few classes every semester as well."

"I don't remember you as being the schooling type."

He chuckled. "True, but I don't want to be a has-been player who spends the rest of his life making a living off his two minutes of fame. I figured a degree of some kind might do me some good."

Interesting. The guy she'd known in college had lived for the limelight. And she'd read all about him in every tabloid after he'd left.

"What are you reading?"

She glanced at the cover of the book. "Dead Awakenings."

He snickered. "A vampire book? I wouldn't take you for one of those vampire girls."

Not that he knew anything about her anymore. "Surprisingly, they're not vampires. It's zombies–Deaders. A girl enters an unsanctioned drug trial to pay some bills and wakes up to find she's become a Deader. It's good."

They stared at each other. Jesse's eyes crinkled in the corners, revealing lines that hadn't been there before. His dark hair had been cut a bit more stylish and the stubble looked good on him. His hazel eyes and crooked grin were exactly the same as she remembered. But his outfit cost more than she remembered his entire wardrobe being worth in college.

Annika's mind screamed at her to invite him to sit down, but her heart told her to send him packing. Walk away with a smile and a 'good to see you'.

"So, what are you up to? Did you become a nurse?"

It surprised her that he even remembered. "No, actually. I–"

"Jesse! There you are." A bombshell blonde dressed like a snow bunny slid up next to him and claimed his arm with hers.

Annika's gut clenched tight at the sight of the perky blonde- the kind of girl she'd always envisioned Jesse would end up with– even on the night that he'd told her he wanted to marry her. Which had been exactly one week before he'd gotten drafted.

"Who's your friend?" she asked through glossy bubblegum lips. The girl couldn't have been more than twenty-five or twenty-six. Annika fought to keep her jealousy at bay, heavens knew she was used to men throwing away the lives they had for women a decade younger. It didn't get any easier though.

"Oh, Carrie, this is an old friend of mine from college, Annika. Annika, this is Carrie."

Time for her to shut the conversation down and move on. "It's nice to meet you," Annika managed.

"We should go, hon. We don't want to be late for our massage appointments." Carrie's southern drawl only added to her charm, making Annika cringe all the more. A beauty queen and her king, perfect. Just what she didn't need to see in the aftermath of her life.

"Yeah." The word came out slow as if he didn't even realize he was saying it. And his eyes never left Annika's face. "It was great to see you." Sincerity punctuated his words making her all the more uncomfortable.

She gave him a tight smile. "You too."

"We should go to lunch, and catch up." He threw her another great smile that threatened to make her say yes.

This was not happening. Warning bells chimed in her head making her gathered up her things and throw them in her bag. She was not going to be drawn back in no matter how charming his smile.

"Why don't you invite her to our Christmas party?" asked Carrie.

"You don't have to do that." Annika stood trying to make her escape.

"It's a great idea," Jesse said. "Here." He pulled

open his messenger bag and removed a card, and handed it to her. "Please, come."

"And bring a guest," Carrie added.

Jesse's smile faltered before he nodded. "Of course."

Annika looked at the linen embossed card and wondered if Carrie had picked them out. "I'll think about it."

"Great." Jesse zipped his coat. "Maybe I'll see you around campus before then."

Annika gave a tight smile. Carrie waved as she walked outside. Jesse stopped suddenly and turned back.

"Hey. I just realized what this is." He held out the potted plant to her. "It's rosemary. You're favorite, right?"

Why did he know that? Why did he remember that?

"Uh... yes. It is."

"You like it in your lemonade."

She nodded, unsure of what to say. He continued to stand there, holding the plant out to her until she took it from him making him smile.

"Thanks," she said through a suddenly dry throat.

"You're welcome."

She needed to stop this. She needed to stop acting like a schoolgirl. "I have to go."

He motioned over his shoulder to Carrie. "Yeah, me too."

Neither moved.

"Please consider coming to the get together," he said.

"We'll see."

Without another word Jesse limped out of the doughnut shop.

Annika's fingers ran circles over the raised print on the card as she watched them hop into a souped-up Land Rover and back out of the snow packed parking spot. Jesse Winchester, the love of her life, was back at Moorpark College.

Dear Reader,

Thank you for taking the time to read *Christmas at Hart's Lodge.* This book was so different from my others. Light and sweet it was definitely a change from my usual dark stuff. I hope you liked reading it as much as I liked writing it.

If you enjoyed the book, please take a moment to leave a review on your favorite retailer. Your reviews make all the difference to an author and the success of books. Feel free to take a moment and email me and let me know what you liked about the book or who your favorite character was and why. I love hearing from readers. It makes writing so much more fun when I hear from my readers.

VampWereZombie@Gmail.com

To find out more about me and my Upcoming Releases, Please Join my Street Team for Swag and Freebies.

I also love connecting with readers! Stalk me everywhere!
I look forward to hearing from you!
Rebekah R. Ganiere - BOOKS WITH A BITE

USA Today Bestselling Author

Rebekah R. Ganiere

Fairelle Series

Red the Were Hunter - Book One

Yanti's Choice - Free Fairelle Short Story

Snow the Vampire Slayer - Book Two

Jamen's Yuletide Bride - Book Three

Zelle and the Tower - Book Four

Cinder the Fae - Book Five

Belle and the Beast - Book Six

Gerall's Festivus Bride - Book Seven

Jak the Giant Healer - Book Eight

Olivia and the Giant - Book Nine (Coming Soon)

Eric's Wayward Bride - Book Ten (Coming Soon)

Wolf River

PROMISED at the Moon

CURSED by the Moon

RECLAIMED from the Moon

TAMED under the Moon

UNLEASHED with the Moon

FATED despite the Moon

FOUND because of the Moon (Coming Soon)

The Society Series

Reign of the Vampires

Rise of the Fae

Vengeance of the Demons

The Otherworlder Series

Kidnapped at Christmas

Vigilante at Valentine

Massacre at Mardi Gras (Coming Soon)

Hoodwinked at Halloween (Coming Soon)

Dead Awakenings

Kissed by the Reaper

Dracula's Bride

Happy Holidays Romances

Newsletter

To claim your Two FREE Books and find out more about Rebekah R. Ganiere and her other Upcoming Releases

You can Go Here:

www.RebekahGaniere.com/Newsletter